# *Postpartum Dead*

BOOK
8

### A CLAIRE BURKE MYSTERY

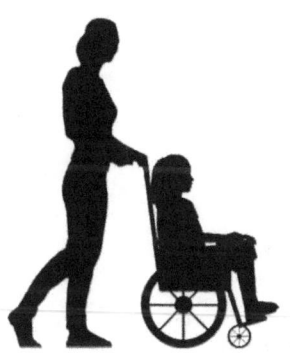

*by*

## Emma Pivato

This book is fiction. All characters, events, and organizations portrayed in this novel are the product of the author's imagination or are used fictitiously. Any resemblance to actual persons— living or dead—is entirely coincidental.

For information, email Cozy Cat Press at:
**cozycatpress@gmail.com**
or visit our website at:
**www.cozycatpress.com**

**COZY CAT**
**P R E S S**

ISBN: 978-1-952579-25-7

Printed in the United States of America

10 9 8 7 6 5 4 3 2 1

Dedication

This book is dedicated to my son, Marcus Pivato
(the inspiration for the Mario character in this series), my
adventurous daughter-in-law, Reem Yassawi, (who has opened
us up to new worlds and ways of being), and my smart, beautiful
grand-daughters, Leila and Aziza Pivato

Acknowledgements

Thank you to my husband, Joe Pivato, who thoroughly
critiqued the manuscript and provided a number of
improvements.

Thank you also to my friend, Kathy Talwar who reviewed an
earlier draft and suggested several useful changes.

Once again, I must thank the kind people at the Super 8 Motel
in North Leduc, who make it so easy for me to be comfortable
there while I do my writing.

# Table of Contents

# List of Characters

Claire Burke and Dan Marchyshyn: married with three children: Jessica—age 16½—and twins Isaac and Isabel—age 4½ months

Tia and Jimmy Elves: married with two children:  Mario—age 14—and Marion——age 2½

Mother-baby group ladies: Ella, Delsie, Betty, Mona, and Valerie

Mona and Stefano Amato and their 8-month-old daughter, Tammy

Rosetta de Felice: Mona's mother and also the mother of Jocelyn de Felice, lawyer

Jason Albright: Jocelyn's husband and the father of their three children

Dr. Marco Amato: Stefano's brother and principal of a bilingual school, and his wife Fiona, an interior designer

Don Marron: young Stefano's "counsellor"

Inspector Don McCoy and Sergeant Al Crombie: Claire's police contacts

The Gordons: Gerry, a financial advisor who works with Stefano, and his wife Nell

Ian Turner, and Sid and Fran Cyber: disgruntled clients of Stefano

Annie: a former "girlfriend" of Stefano

# - 1 -

## Claire Joins a Group

Claire felt her face heating up as she scanned the circle of young mothers in the room. The director of the mother-baby program had just asked her to share her story, since this was her first visit.

*What can I say?* she asked herself desperately. These other mothers are probably all professionals on maternity leave from their offices——and who am I? I'm only on maternity leave because I quit my not so professional position.

"My name is Claire Burke," she stuttered, "and these are my four-month old twins, Isaac and Isabel——Ike and Izzie for short." There was some giggling in the room after that remark and Claire imagined that the other mothers were laughing at her. They were all so much younger and must be wondering what a 42-year-old like her was even doing there.

"I also have a 16-year old-daughter, Jessica, and as you might imagine, the twins were a bit of a surprise." There was open laughter at that point, and Claire then realized that they were laughing with her, not at her, and involuntarily sighed in relief. Isaac had been sleeping in the carrier on her back and cried out briefly at this point before dozing off again. Isabel shifted on her lap.

"Until a month before their birth," Claire went on, "I was running a home for three adults with various developmental disabilities, but it has now been taken over by somebody else. I don't have any plans yet for what I'm going to do when the twins are older, but I want to go back to work."

Claire stopped talking at that point and was welcomed warmly by the others who must have seen her as an interesting anomaly. During the coffee break, a number of them came up to her and asked her questions, and Claire relaxed and began to feel more comfortable. But she still didn't know what she was doing there.

Later that evening, Claire shared her feelings with her ever-patient husband, Dan. "I don't know who I am anymore besides just being a mother," she complained.

"Just a mother?" he replied. "Just a mother in her '40's with infant twins and a 16-year-old daughter with profound disabilities who's as happy and healthy as she can be considering all her problems?" He threw his hands in the air to emphasize his point.

"Fine. I get your point——but the twins aren't going to be babies forever and Jessie is going to become part of the adult care system and probably go into a community living home soon because that will be the only way we can access government service for her after she turns 18. Then what? I have no idea what I'm going to do with the rest of my life."

"Well, you could apply for a private investigator license or go to the police training academy and work toward becoming a detective——give Inspector McCoy a run for his money," Dan said jokingly. He was alluding to the various murders Claire had been involved in solving over the past several years, along with her friend, Tia, and to the sometimes irascible detective she'd worked with or against at one time or another, depending on the circumstances. And these were not all your garden variety shootings and stabbings. One had involved a burning car and another, a push off a balcony.

Claire said nothing but looked at him resentfully. She'd been expecting a little compassion to help her deal with her existential angst. Dan quickly picked up on this and went on in a more sympathetic tone. "Look, Claire. The work you've done for Roscoe and Bill and Mavis over the past few years is wonderful. You've literally given them a life, just as you've done for Jessie. And you've organized things so carefully and well that the lifestyles you've established for them are now allowing them to carry on without you. You actually worked yourself out of a job and that's a sign of success, not failure."

Yeah, sure ... but what about now? They don't need me anymore. Who am I now?"

"There are others like them out there," Dan replied, munching on a McIntosh apple from B.C., his favorite. "And then there's the cookbook you've always talked about writing. What about that?"

"I don't know about that. I'm not that great a cook."

"Well, you've had your share of flops. But that's only because you can never seem to follow a recipe without tampering with it. And when you do create something special, you never remember to write it down so you can repeat it a second time. But you can change that behavior if you want to. As Aristotle said, 'virtue is habit.'"

Claire replied defensively, "If I didn't 'tamper', as you say, I wouldn't have been able to create some of those special recipes and I would never have generated all those ideas to help Jessie eat safely despite her swallowing difficulties."

"I know that. You get full marks for ingenuity. All I'm saying is that if you can harness that ingenuity with a measure of self-discipline and organization you should be able to get a cookbook out of it that could help a lot of people like Jessie to have a better quality of life. After all, food is something we can all enjoy no matter what our problems are."

Claire had nothing more to say after this, and just then Isaac woke up demanding attention. After he was settled for the night, it was time for them to go to bed so that brought their problem-solving session to an end.

# - 2 -

## The Present Tense

It was the next Tuesday and Claire awoke at 6:30 in the morning to the sounds of Isaac's cries. She quickly snatched him from his crib before he could wake his sister and held him to her breast to nurse. Having successfully quieted him in this manner, she walked into the kitchen with him and warmed an already prepared bottle. Isaac was still not able to nurse as well as Isabel, and tired quickly. Isabel, on the other hand, nursed eagerly and only accepted a bottle if she had no choice and was still hungry.

Claire congratulated herself on this "Jack Spratt" turn of affairs: two children with such opposite tastes. Because of that, there was always breast milk left over for Isaac when his hunger was satisfied by the bottle, but he still needed some comforting. And Isabel could drink her fill most of the time and a bottle would always be there for her if she needed it. Claire knew that breast milk had beneficial effects on the immune system, so with this strategy she felt she was covering all the bases. And to prove her point, at his last check-up, Isaac had actually weighed a few ounces more than Isabel and both of them had remained healthy.

One of the reasons for the twins' good health, considering that they'd been born in October just at the onset of flu season, is that Claire rarely took them out. Even when they had attended the mother-baby group the day before, she hadn't let them down onto the floor where several other children were crawling around. She'd noticed the other women eying her and judging her over-protectiveness, but this didn't bother Claire. Those women didn't have a Jessie in their lives. They didn't realize how much could be lost and how bad it could get.

Claire's ruminations were interrupted at that point by a tell-tale sound from Jessie's room. Clutching Isaac and the bottle, she glanced through Jessie's door and immediately saw what was happening. She ran to her bedroom and shook her husband awake. As soon as he opened his eyes, she handed Isaac and the bottle to him. "Grand mal; blue lips", she hissed, and then raced for the oxygen tank and from there on to Jessie's bedroom.

The huge convulsive jerks of a fully generalized seizure were now subsiding, but Jessie's lips were growing ominously dark and it was clear that she had stopped breathing. With practiced precision, Claire deftly applied the facemask to Jessie's face. It was attached to a bagger that was in turn fed by an oxygen tank. Claire turned the oxygen on to "Full" and began rhythmically pumping the oxygen into Jessie's lungs. She squeezed the bagger twice, then counted to five and repeated the process several more times. Within a few seconds, Jessie's lips began to regain their natural color, but when Claire stopped squeezing the bagger to see if Jessie would now breathe in on her own, they darkened again.

This process went on for a couple of minutes with Claire gradually reducing the bagger use to one squeeze every five seconds and lowering the oxygen level. At that point, Claire could see that Jessie was beginning to breathe on her own. However, her hands and fingernails were still somewhat dark, so Claire left the oxygen on at this low level for another minute or two but no longer used the bagger. Finally, she removed the oxygen, cleaned the face mask and put the oxygen trolley with its various attachments away.

At this point, Jessie was in a "post-ictal" state, meaning that she was only semi-conscious and was on her way to drifting off to sleep. Claire phoned the special school bus number she'd been given to cancel Jessie's pick-up for the day and then called her after-school assistant to see if she could come in earlier. She could not, so Claire mentally adjusted her plans.

Dan was now at her side, holding the newly awakened Isabel out to Claire to be nursed. Claire took her and said, "I was going to take the twins to this new group I discovered. It's meeting today at eleven, only a couple of blocks from here." Claire looked at Dan hopefully, silently asking him to watch Jessie during that time since he was often able to work from home.

"I'm sorry, Claire. I have an important client meeting at the office. I can't reschedule."

# - 3 -

## Claire Finds a Way

When Claire got an idea in her head, it was very hard for her to let go of it, so she grimly proceeded to get everything done that had to be done before they could all leave for the morning outing. She changed and nursed Isabel and then laid her down. Isaac had already gone back to sleep. Then Claire wiggled the lift sling under Jessie and hoisted her up and onto the commode that sat next to her bed. Once again, she gave silent thanks for the presence of a ceiling lift. Until a few years ago, they'd only had a cumbersome floor lift. Claire had often ignored it and done the lifting herself, and that had not done good things for her back.

The next task was to get Jessie's breakfast ready and after that there was more feeding, washing, dressing and bathroom needs for the children. Somewhere along the line Claire managed to gulp down two cups of coffee and get dressed herself, and by 20 to eleven they were out the door. Isaac was in a baby carrier on Claire's back and Isabel was seated on Jessie's lap and tightly bound to her with a large cloth sling of the type women still use in many parts of the world to tie babies securely to themselves as they go about their work. Claire had also placed a thick tuque on

Isabel's head so when Jessie drooled it would not get her hair wet.

Claire backed Jessie's wheelchair carefully down the ramp and realized that at that point she was sweating. She was grateful for the crisp January air and very pleased with herself for having managed to make it out the door in time despite the heavy odds. But halfway to her destination she had another thought. What if the place wasn't wheelchair accessible? This possibility had not even crossed her mind before, but now she realized what a problem it would be. She soldiered on anyway, frequently flicking her eyes towards Isabel to make sure that the double knotted scarf hadn't somehow loosened and placed her daughter at risk of falling.

Three-quarters of the way there, Claire came to a major intersection with a relatively short traffic light. She was just wondering how the four of them could make it safely across in the time allotted, when a man appeared at her side and asked if he could assist her by pushing the chair across. Claire thanked him gratefully without a moment of anxiety about handing her two daughters over to a total stranger. However, they arrived safely at the other side and, when Claire turned to thank him and take charge of the wheelchair once more, she suddenly realized that in all the morning chaos she'd forgotten to brush her teeth.

Once she resumed her trek, Claire fumbled in her purse with one hand until she found some gum and by that time, they were approaching the host's house, according to the address she'd been given. Claire saw at once that it was not accessible from the front and could only hope that there would be a patio door or back door closer to ground level. She parked the chair at the base of the stairs and then climbed up to ring the bell.

A cheerful-looking middle-aged woman with long, prematurely greying hair opened the door, took in the situation at a glance and smiled warmly at Claire. "Don't worry, dear," she said without further preamble. Then she called over her shoulder to someone inside to put on her boots and help out. She did the same, then marched purposefully down the steps and quickly untied the knots in the scarf restraining Isabel. She handed her to the woman who'd come to help. "This is Betty, by the way," she announced, turning to Claire, "and I'm Ella."

"Claire," Claire responded, taken aback. Then, systematically pointing her finger, she identified Jessie, Isabel and Isaac.

Turning back to Betty, Ella said, "Take Isabel in and give her to Delsie. Then come back and help me carry Jessie up," she ordered. Turning back to Claire, she said "You look exhausted. Grab your bag and go on in. Get a chair ready for her, whichever you think is best. If somebody's in it, just kick them out."

Claire retrieved the 'lift strap' from Jessie's bag and handed it to Betty who'd returned by that time. Ella was busy undoing the restraint straps on Jessie's 'butterfly vest', a four-point tie-down that kept her secured in the chair. After she finished, Claire demonstrated how the lift strap worked. It was a single, six-inch wide band of tough, reinforced denim that Dan had devised, and Claire quickly slid it under Jessie's legs. Dan and Claire had used this two-person lift system to transfer Jessie on their various trips with her through the years to Mexico——the mountains and the occasional visits to relatives at other places in Canada and the United States.

Claire pointed out the lift handles, mimicking the stance she took to support Jessie safely in the sling with one hand on the lift handle by her leg and one hand behind her shoulder. After one last worried look backward, Claire headed up the steps with the bag. She knew all too well the devastation that could result if Jessie ever fell as she had no protective reflexes. However, there was an air of efficiency about Ella that reassured her, and she saw that Ella was carefully instructing her lifting partner, Betty, on safe hand and shoulder placement for her to use the sling on the opposite side. In the meantime, Jessie was thoroughly enjoying all the attention from these new people and making happy sounds.

Claire walked through the door, deposited her boots and coat in the foyer and headed hesitantly into the living room where three other women were already seated. Three babies were playing with blocks and some minicars and trucks on the floor and Isabel was also sitting on the floor propped up against the base of the sofa and watching the proceedings with interest. Claire asked the woman sitting behind her whom she took to be Delsie, if she'd lift Isaac out of her back sling and place him on the rug beside Isabel. Somehow, Claire felt okay about this. It was not the same kind of unhygienic setting as the other, larger mother-baby group she'd attended the day before. That space was a school gym heavily used by various classes.

Claire scanned the room and noted a woman seated on an oversized love seat with reclining seats, holding a rather oversized baby. She saw at once that it was the ideal place for Jessie to be seated, and she also saw why the person sitting there had chosen it. The person was very overweight herself and needed the extra space to spread out. Claire looked uncertainly at her and she looked back with a slight air of defiance but Claire just stood there and pulled a three-foot square pad from her bag. By this time, Jessie was on her way in. Then another mother jumped up from a comfortable-looking armchair and addressed the woman on the sofa cheerfully.

"Sit here with the baby, Mona. It'll be more supportive for you anyway. Mona raised herself grudgingly and shambled over. Claire carefully placed the pad in the middle of the loveseat and motioned to Ella and Betty to seat Jessie there. Then she sat down on Jessie's right side and the former armchair occupier, a slender and wiry-looking person, moved over and sat down on her left. "Hello," she said to Claire. "My name's Valerie, but you can call me Val. What's your name?"

"This is Jessie and I'm Claire," Claire said warmly. "Thanks for helping out with the seating. It's a tricky process placing Jessie safely anywhere else but her chair. Somebody has to then sit beside her at all times to keep her from falling."

"Well, we'll just take turns getting up and that way she'll stay safe and we can still move around when we need to," Val replied.

Claire smiled at her gratefully and opened her mouth to say something else, but just then Ella took over. First, she introduced the other women to Claire: Delsie, Mona and Betty and the various children in the room. Then she announced the theme for the day's session. "Today, we'll be discussing mother-baby isolation and exploring some ways to deal with it. Let's start by sharing how this affects each of us." She turned to Mona, now ensconced in the armchair but still looking a bit miffed as if she'd been cheated out of something.

"Tell us about your situation, Mona. Are you feeling kind of alone and cut off or are you managing okay with your social life?"

"Oh, I'm definitely cut off," Mona responded emphatically. "Once my husband leaves for work in the morning, Tammy and I are all alone." She pointed toward the baby now sleeping in her capacious lap. "I don't drive, you see, and I have to walk two blocks to even get to a bus stop. And you know how windy it's been here lately. Tammy hates that and she just cries all the time when I try to take her out. And then when we finally do get on the bus, I often end up having to hold her in my lap because there's a wheelchair parked in the cart space."

Claire wanted to point out that the tie-down space was actually designated for wheelchairs but managed to say nothing. *Tia would be pleased about that*, she thought, referring to her best friend and sleuthing partner. But, glancing towards the door, Claire got upset all over again. She just knew that the monster-sized cart lolling there belonged to Mona and her already overweight baby.

Claire had had her own bitter experiences in the past with having to let buses pass her by because a cart was occupying the wheelchair space. She'd finally got up the nerve to march onto the bus with the wheelchair anyway, and stare at the offending mother as she stood there. If the mother didn't take the hint and move, she then approached the driver who was obliged to ask the woman to relinquish the wheelchair slot. If he didn't agree to intervene in the situation, she stood in the aisle with the wheelchair brakes on, lurching from side to side until everyone on the bus became uncomfortable and the social pressure from other passengers finally forced the woman to move.

On one occasion she had informed the driver when leaving that she'd taken his number and would be reporting him to his superiors. Of course, there was payback for this. A couple of times after that, when the same driver came along and saw her waiting alone at the stop with her daughter, he'd passed her by. And when Jessie's support staff needed to take the bus, they didn't have the nerve to become confrontational in this way. As a result, there were times when Jessie ended up significantly late for whatever activity was on the agenda for that day. But Claire had learned the hard way to pick her battles, because too many times she'd lost the war by speaking too freely. Therefore, on this occasion, she chose to say nothing.

Mona went on speaking then. Although not strictly on topic, she complained in a whiny voice about how much work it was to look after her daughter and how her mother, who was not working, was rarely available to assist due to her own social activities or a previous commitment to helping Mona's sister who had three young children.

As Mona was winding down, a couple of hands went up in the air from other mothers eager to offer helpful suggestions. However, Ella didn't acknowledge them, stating instead that she'd go around the room first so everyone had a chance to share and then there would be time for discussion. She was sure several of the mothers who were present had similar feelings of isolation and there wouldn't be time to spend on repeating the same advice over and over. "I think we should move on to our new guests today and see what mother Claire has to say," Ella concluded.

Claire felt a moment of spiteful glee, recalling what Tia had said about timing being everything. She now had an opportunity to place Mona's evident self-pity and her insensitivity to the needs of others in perspective. Claire then told the story of their morning in a matter-of-fact manner. She went on to describe how she found it difficult to travel more than a couple of blocks because of the seating arrangement in her van that kept the twins too far away from her. "We have a 7-seater van adapted to accommodate Jessie's wheelchair where the middle seats usually are. That's why the twins have to be in the far back seat. The twins and I could use the bus during the day when Jessie's at school," Claire went on. The stop is quite near our house and I've tried it out a couple of times with them. But it's really difficult placing a double stroller on the bus. It blocks the aisle and become a safety hazard for everyone. In fact," she added slyly, "all the new over-sized strollers have that problem." Claire studiously avoided looking towards the door but saw the eyes of several others stealthily shifting in that direction.

Once again, Ella moved directly on to another mother without allowing time for question or comment. After everyone had shared, the comments began in earnest. The first two questions were directed at Claire. "Have you considered using DATS?" Betty asked.

Claire looked at her and smiled. "Our Edmonton DATS stands for 'Disabled Adult Transportation System' and Jessie isn't yet eligible, although she will be in a year and a half when she turns 18. But even then," Claire went on, "it wouldn't work for us because I'd have the twins with me. Only one other rider is allowed on the bus with a DATS user and then only as an attendant if the user is too disabled to manage on their own, like Jessie.

At that point Delsie suggested, "Could your husband drive the van to work and give you the car during the day when Jessie is at school?"

"I suppose that might work," Claire said thoughtfully. "We'd have to get special fittings in the base of the back seat to hold the car seats and it would be a bit of a hassle moving them back and forth to the van if we wanted to go out with Jessie on the weekend. But it could work. Thanks for the idea, Delsie," Claire added brightly.

Claire observed that Mona was looking increasingly annoyed and decided she'd talked enough. There was a temporary lull and then the other two women with babies were offered some helpful suggestions with regard to their particular situations.

Finally, Val turned to Mona. "Have you thought about asking your mother to agree to a set time each week to help you so she could arrange her schedule accordingly?"

"As if she would," Mona sneered. "The first time something more interesting came along she'd cancel on me."

Betty chimed in at this point. "Maybe you and your sister could swap babysitting mornings once a week to give each of you a break."

"And be stuck with her three brats in exchange? I don't think so. It would take me a week to recover after that."

There was an awkward pause and Mona started organizing herself and the baby to leave, a faintly disgusted look on her face. Ella interjected at that point, the first time she'd spoken since opening the group up to questions. "Mona, you seem really unhappy. It's possible that you might be struggling with postpartum depression. I have a card here for a counselling helpline. I wish you'd call them and talk to someone just to be on the safe side. Postpartum depression is due to a biochemical imbalance after childbirth and is more common than most people realize."

Mona stood up at that point looking very angry. She stalked over to the cart, plopped Tammy down in the seat, and began wrestling with the tie-down straps. When she was ready to leave, she turned to the group. "I see what's happening here" she said. "You're all trying to say that it's my fault. Meanwhile, some newbie comes in and tells a sad story and you all get sucked in."

Mona glared at Claire. "Well, I know when I'm not wanted. You all have a good life," she sneered. And with that, Mona and Tammy were gone, the door slamming behind them.

The rest of the group sat in stunned silence, listening to the wheels of the cart as they bumped violently down the steps. Finally, Delsie asked meekly, "Shouldn't we have said something to stop her——not let her leave like that? What if she is clinically depressed? You see all those ads about preventing suicide——or even murder/suicide in some cases. What if she does something to herself——and the baby?"

There was a collective intake of breath as the group took in the potential horror of the situation. But Ella was shaking her head. "No. Mona wasn't ready to hear anybody. There's nothing we could have said or done that would have made a difference. I did manage to slip the counselling card into her bag and when she calms down and finds it maybe she will call. Maybe not——but it's all any of us could do at this point. People have to be ready to seek help before you can help them."

# - 4 -

## Claire Makes a Friend

After the meeting, Val hoisted her nine-month-old son, Jeffrey, into her backpack carrier and offered to walk Claire home. "That's a lot for you to manage," she declared. "It would be safer if you had someone with you just in case anything goes wrong."

Claire agreed gratefully and then, after reflecting a moment, asked, "Would you like to stay for lunch? I have some left-over homemade quiche that's pretty good."

"That would be great," Val agreed. "I have nowhere else to be except home, changing diapers, washing dishes and trying to avoid turning on the afternoon soaps so I don't go stir-crazy."

Val and Jeffrey were both very happy with the crustless quiche Claire had prepared, and Val was surprised that it had no pieces too big for Jeffrey to manage. Claire was appropriately gratified and commented, "It's one of the recipes that I plan to include in my cookbook."

"Oh?" Val asked. "What's it going to be called?"

"Gourmet Purée. I'm working on it for Jessie and others who need it. You might be surprised how many people have great difficulty chewing for one reason or another. But Dan and I have always said if we wouldn't eat something, then Jessie shouldn't either. Therefore, we don't just turn food into mush for her. We want Jessie to have positive culinary experiences. Her world is limited enough as it is without limiting it unnecessarily."

"Well, if your other recipes are as good as this, then I'm in. How about writing it down for me while I take Jeffrey in the bedroom and change him?"

"Uh, I'll email it to you when I get a minute," Claire replied, always one to procrastinate.

"No, please do it now. The twins are sleeping, Jessie looks happy, and I really, really want to try making it. Cooking's not my thing, but it looks like a recipe I could manage——and I know my husband would love it."

Claire agreed, pulled out her laptop, and began typing but it took a long time. Finally, Val started reading it over her shoulder and was surprised to see that Claire was adding other recipes. Claire interpreted her unspoken question and told her, "I never think in terms of a recipe. What's the point of that? I imagine complete meals. That makes more sense to me." True to her word, Claire had added recipes for tomato-basil salad and stir-fried green beans with garlic.

She had been about to type out one of her most successful multi-grain bread recipes to round out what was in her mind a complete meal when Val stopped her. "I can barely cook," she said. "There's no way I'm ever going to make bread, and looking at the recipe for it will just make me feel guilty and inadequate. But I must say, you make it all sound so easy."

"Cooking is easy. You just have to have what cognitive psychologists call a 'mental map':  your starting point, steps along the way and your end point."

"Sure, but what exactly are those steps?"

"First you organize your ingredients and equipment, second, you plan out the order in which to do things so that, third, you reach the end point together. With the beans, for example, you don't heat the oil in the pan and then start peeling and slicing the garlic, and you don't put the garlic in the pan and then run to the freezer to root out the green beans. The garlic and beans and seasonings are there ready to go before the pan gets hot. Don't you ever watch cooking shows?"

"Who has time? In fact, who has time to cook when you have little kids. I generally just end up throwing something together or buying prepared stuff."

"Well, it helps if you like to eat. Cooking is much more motivating that way. I always feel sorry for men with very thin wives. As you can see, I like to eat——but our main motivation is Jessie. We really love to see her enjoying her food."

"But I don't see you giving her these green beans, unless you cook them to death. It would be too hard to purée them."

"We do give them to her. In fact, they're one of her favorites. But you're right. Green beans and asparagus require a special, two-step process to prepare them for her. First, I have to grind them as fine as I can in the food processor. Then, I transfer them with the help of a silicone spatula to our Vitamix blender and it does the rest. In less than a minute I'm left with a velvety puree."

"I've tried making baby food in the blender and it's a messy, wasteful process that requires a lot of liquid to even work," Val complained.

"That's why you have to use the processor with the wider base first, so the food won't get stuck. And it's also important to have high power machines. Cheap machines with less power just won't work."

"My blender is pretty good, but I still end up with a lot of food wrapped around the blades that I can't get out. It's a very wasteful process."

"Well, Dan and I laugh about that. There are times when Jessie ends up eating our leftovers. The beans are a good example. It's too complicated to get the beans on the table just when they're hot and tender-crisp and at their best, and still prepare them properly for Jessie. Thus, we often give them to her the next day after I've had time to process them. But, in turn, we often eat Jessie's leftovers because after I use the processor and blender and get out all the puree I can with a spatula, I then whir the residue around with a little fresh water to clean the blades. I pour the results into a large container I store in the freezer for making soup. Then I just whir the machines again with hot water and soap, rinse them out, and store them in the dish rack to dry. No fuss, no muss, no bother."

"Pretty cool," Val said, admiringly. "Are you that efficient with house cleaning, as well?"

"Not even close," Claire replied, glancing at the dust on her baseboards and hoping that Val would not notice. "I never did get that particular mental map. Luckily, my husband, Dan, is quite patient with me about my casual housecleaning. On the other hand, he hates my cookbook title, *Gourmet Purée*. He claims it demeans the good quality of the food we prepare for her. I've tried to tell him that there would be no point in me trying to publish a cookbook if it weren't for this particular niche market. There are thousands of interesting, creative cookbooks out there already and no need for one more from a quirky, fly-by-the-seat-of-your-pants cook like me."

# - 5 -

## The Lull Before the Storm

The next two months passed calmly. It was now late April, and the twins, who'd been born October the 3rd were 6½ months old––or 6 months if you took into account that they were born prematurely. Dan and Claire were no longer experiencing the grinding exhaustion that had characterized the first few months of the twins' existence and the Marchyshyn household was falling into a regular routine.

Claire had continued to attend the nearby mother-baby group and had even brought Jessie along on several occasions, as she'd been warmly invited to do. However, Jessie's teacher complained about her absenteeism since the school was still paying for a full-time assistant for her. Claire could understand this, but also saw how much more Jessie seemed to enjoy her times with a group of adult women and young children than she enjoyed her school setting.

Jessie was now in a grade-eleven class, and it was evident that at this stage in their lives the other students were fully occupied with fitting into their peer group and meeting their academic requirements. They had little time or energy left over to bother with Jessie and she was becoming increasingly isolated. Claire was aware of this and a plan was beginning to form in her mind, but she was not yet ready to talk about it——not even with Dan.

The mother meetings had quickly become the highlight of Claire's week and she was soon recognized as the group guru when preparing baby food was the topic of discussion. But many other topics were mulled over at the weekly meetings that Claire found to be personally very helpful to her. Together they explored issues like: how and where to exercise with baby in tow, which stores had the best washrooms and areas set aside for changing and nursing babies, what books were most useful in escaping mother guilt, finding ways to meet both mother and baby needs, and so on.

Occasionally during the meetings, Mona's abrupt departure had been recalled by one or another of the women, who wondered if they ought to reach out to her. Ella admitted that, despite what she'd said initially about not being able to help her until she was ready, she had tried to contact Mona once, but had the phone slammed in her ear. The Mona issue seemed to wane then without any firm plan in place and the group moved on to other matters of more immediate interest to the various members.

It was now the last Tuesday in April and Claire got up in a happy mood, knowing what lay ahead of her. She sent Jessie off to school regretfully, not wanting to rile the teacher up any further. Claire comforted herself by recalling the letter she had had just mailed to the school superintendent, someone with whom she had a mutual respect and understanding. Then she had readied herself and the twins for the exciting morning that lay ahead of them.

Claire slipped on her favorite pair of trousers and noted that they were becoming loose at the waist. She was doing more and more walking with the twins in their double stroller while Jessie was at school. Sometimes she even walked down into the Whitemud Ravine, an Edmonton City Park near their home. And the effects on her waistline were beginning to show. They reached Ella's house just on time and the other group members were already there and settled in. Claire greeted them cheerfully, but they didn't return her smile. Instead she was confronted by a sea of shocked and guilty faces.

"Haven't you heard?" Val asked. "It was on the 9 o'clock news. Mona and her husband were killed last night. News reporters are speculating that it's a case of murder-suicide, just like that case in Toronto in 2014 where that rich pharmacist and his wife were found dead by their family pool."

"Oh, no!" Claire gasped. "What about the baby? What about Tammy?"

"Apparently, she was staying with Mona's mother. That is what one neighbour said anyway. The police, as usual, aren't talking so everything's up in the air at this point," Betty offered.

"Then where did the press get the idea that it was murder-suicide?"

"Reporters managed to interview several of the neighbours before they were stopped by the police," Betty explained. "Two or three of these neighbours apparently mentioned that they often heard loud arguments between Stefano and Mona coming from the Amato's house and that she seemed to be the main instigator."

"But who found the bodies and how were they placed? That's what we need to find out," Claire contributed, snapping into amateur detective mode. Some vigorous speculating ensued but one person was not actively participating in this discussion. Ella sat off in one corner of the room, her face white and her lips trembling. Claire saw this and quickly deposited the twins on the floor before going to her. Val started taking their coats off, apparently grateful for something concrete to do.

"Don't look like that," Claire begged. "It's not your fault, Ella. You couldn't have known. And besides," she went on, "there's no proof at this point that it was murder-suicide. It could have been just plain murder, and if so, it's just a lucky break that

Tammy was with her grand-mother."

"But we don't know," Ella replied. "We should have continued to reach out to her. I should have made more of an effort."

Ella left the room then and they heard her bedroom door closing behind her. They could hear her crying and at that point, Claire decided she needed to take charge. She knew grief; she knew loss; she knew murder——and it was up to her to get the group back on track.

Claire talked to the others about the cases she'd been involved in and how often things turned out in a very different way than anyone working on it had expected. A few minutes later, Ella crept out of her room and sat down quietly in the same corner she'd occupied previously. She huddled there, looking like only a shadow of her former cheerful, take-charge self.

Claire turned to her and said, "Look, Ella. We can't change what happened, but we can do our best to ensure that whoever murdered Mona and her husband is brought to justice."

Ella looked at her in surprise and spoke for the first time. "But what if she's the murderer?"

"It's possible, but not likely," Claire said briskly. "If Mona could be that unpleasant to us, I'm sure she was equally unpleasant to others and made a few enemies along the way. And we don't know anything about her or her husband. You are the one who mentioned postpartum depression to her, and I thought you were just throwing that out there to give her something to hang onto to save face. She never struck me as depressed——and I have a very dear friend who recently went through a severe depression after a miscarriage. Mona came across as angry and self-pitying and kind of nasty——not depressed."

There was a collective gasp from the group at this point, its members clearly enculturated in the notion that you must never speak ill of the dead. "Okay," Claire acknowledged. "That was harsh. But if we're going to find Mona's killer we need to start with as clear and accurate a picture of her as possible, not some rose-colored one."

Claire saw Val's lip twitch at this point and was reminded sadly of Tia. Tia was too busy these days with her demanding job, her 2½–year-old-daughter, her precocious son, now 14 years old and rapidly outgrowing what high school had to offer, and her demanding husband to have any time left over to help with this latest mystery. But in the past couple of months, Claire and Val had grown quite close. *With Val's help and perhaps the help of some of the others, we can do this*, Claire thought to herself.

Claire then continued with her inner ruminations for a few moments. It was often the case that when a new idea caught her up, it took her several minutes thereafter to unwind her line of reasoning. She hadn't liked Mona although she certainly hadn't wished her dead. Under normal circumstances she would have let this murder pass her by, especially after faithfully promising Dan to be a good little mother and focus on raising her children properly.

*But this situation is different,* Claire reasoned in an effort to justify the actions she was about to undertake. She had come to really admire and care for Ella, and it was gut-wrenching to see her so reduced. Claire felt that if she didn't solve this murder, Ella would spend the rest of her life staggering under a burden of guilt.

# - 6 -

## First Steps

Claire awoke the next morning with a new energy. Dan commented on how bright and cheerful she looked, but she didn't share her inner thoughts with him. Firstly, it would appear macabre to be energized by somebody's murder, and secondly, he'd be very upset about her plans to get involved in finding the murderer.

Dan was already up and getting Jessie dressed for school. He'd recently taken over with Jessie in the mornings so Claire could get the twins up and changed and dressed and fed. It was impossible to meet the needs of all three children at the same time, and there was a strict deadline for getting Jessie ready to go: the 8:15 arrival of the school wheelchair bus. Dan had worked out this new arrangement at his office and, as a result was arriving home later in the evenings on the days he didn't work from home.

Dan was an architect working for a large firm that had recently relocated to the new Stantec Tower in downtown Edmonton. At 66 stories, it was now the tallest building in Western Canada and held many comfortable amenities including a high-end coffee bar to serve the people who worked there. However, getting there involved a time-consuming commute, and Dan was glad he was able to work from home a couple of days a week. Claire didn't even want to think about how much harder life with Jessie would have been through the years without the extra support Dan was able to provide. It was Jessie's strict school schedule that created the boot camp atmosphere in their home every weekday, and Claire wondered again what answer she would receive back from the school superintendent. Right now, however, she had other things to worry about and as she worked through the early morning routine with Isaac and Isabel, she mulled over what her next steps should be.

Later, when Jessie and Dan were both gone for the day and the twins were down for their mid-morning nap, Claire had her first opportunity to sit down and relax for a little while with her coffee and newspaper. A quick scan through the front section of the *Edmonton Journal* provided no further information on the deaths of Mona and her husband, except that she now knew that his name was Stefano Amato and Mona's maiden name was de Felice.

The names sounded Italian to Claire and she'd need to ask Tia if she knew from what region or regions they originated. Tia's parents were from the south of Italy, Calabria, and Tia, whose name was short for Tiziana, was proud of her Italian roots and quite knowledgeable about Italian history and geography in general.

A quick check on the obituary column indicated that the names of the two victims were not yet there. Claire then checked on-line under Edmonton addresses to see if there were listings under either surname. Strangely, there was nothing for a Stefano Amato but there was a listing for a Rosetta de Felice. *Perhaps that's Mona's mother,* Claire thought. Should I call her? She must be terribly upset and why would she want to hear from a total stranger at a time like this? Claire contemplated calling Val to ask her opinion, but just then she heard a noise from the twin's room and her mothering day began again, leaving no more time for sleuthing.

The next day, Dan was able to work at home so Claire had a little more time to herself but considerably less opportunity for working on the murder. She did manage to re-check the listing for Rosetta de Felice and found to her surprise that the address given was only about 12 blocks from her house. That afternoon, she decided to take the twins for a brisk walk, as it was a balmy 16 degrees Celsius (63 degrees Fahrenheit), which was pretty good for early May in Edmonton. As she walked, pushing the double stroller with Isaac and Isabel nestled inside, still in their winter jackets and boots, she marveled to herself that she wouldn't even have attempted this a couple of years ago. Her consistent gym activity over the past two years, although only twice a week for the most part, had made a definite difference for the better to her overall fitness level and also to her weight.

As Claire approached Rosetta's house, she wondered what to do. *I can just check it out from the outside, see if it is well kept or run down, note what kind of car she has if it happens to be in the driveway. That will tell me something.* But even as she said this, Claire knew that after walking twelve long blocks to get there this wouldn't be enough to satisfy her.

Claire was ruminating so hard that she almost missed the house, but then she noted the mailbox set on a post at the bottom of the steps. In clear letters on the outside of the mailbox was the name, de Felice. Just then, a woman opened the door and stepped outside. Since she wasn't wearing a coat or boots, Claire guessed that she was about to retrieve the mail and she turned the cart sharply up the walk, almost tipping it over in the process. The woman turned towards her in surprise and smiled tentatively as Claire approached.

"Excuse me," Claire said. "I couldn't help noticing the name on your mailbox. My name is Claire Burke and I was once in a group with a Mona de Felice. Is she a relative of yours?"

"She is——was——my daughter," the woman replied. "What do you want?"

"I——I just wanted to express my condolences," Claire replied. "I heard about what happened."

The woman stared at her wordlessly and Claire went on talking. "I, we…the other group members and me, that is…we all felt sorry when she left our group and wondered how she was getting on. The group leader even called her once, but Mona didn't want to talk to her." The woman continued staring.

Claire blundered on, fervently wishing she could channel Tia, who was much better at this type of delicate exchange. But Claire had her own gift. She could speak directly from the heart without filtering her words through the layers of social niceties that sometimes smothered and muted the verbal exchanges of others in these circumstances. "Look!" she said. "We're all feeling really awful… shocked and sad and guilty. We keep wondering if we should have done more to try to get her back, or if we could have done more to support her in some way. We don't even know what really happened and the press is talking about possible murder-suicide."

Rosetta winced when Claire said this and turned away. Claire impulsively let go of the cart and rushed over to put her arms around her. But the woman, who was now facing Claire and looking outward, shook her off and pointed. "Look! The cart!" she cried. Claire turned to see the cart sliding backwards down the walk and towards the busy road. She rushed madly to retrieve it just as a car whizzed past. Shakily, she pushed it back towards Rosetta, her face blanched white.

"You'd better come in," Rosetta said. "Here! Give me one and you take the other. The cart can stay here. Just put the brakes on this time."

Claire did as she was told, fumbling to undo the straps because she was still shaky and therefore uncoordinated. She handed Isabel, who she always saw as the stronger, calmer one, to Rosetta, and cradled Isaac in her arms, managing to grab the diaper bag off the back quickly with one hand before returning it to a support position under Isaac. She mounted the steps slowly and carefully, still in shock.

Rosetta deposited Isabel on the rug in what was clearly the living room and then turned back to the door and held out her arms to take Isaac, motioning to the closet. Claire took off her coat and boots as quickly as she could before joining them. She sat down on the sofa without waiting to be invited and reached over to pick up Isaac. She clutched him firmly, a look of guilt and horror on her face as she contemplated what could have happened.

Rosetta just sat looking at her and finally she said, "You look as if you could use a cup of tea and maybe a couple of cookies. You've had quite a shock."

"Thank you," Claire said fervently, and it was clear she wasn't thinking of the tea and cookies but of what could have—probably would have—happened if Rosetta hadn't noticed what was happening and alerted Claire when she did.

When Rosetta came back with the Earl Gray tea and digestive biscuits, she placed the whole tea tray on the table in front of Claire and motioned to her to help herself. She sat down across from her guest and looked at her wordlessly. Claire felt judged. She nodded her thanks and helped herself to some tea before speaking. Notably, she added nothing to it and ignored the biscuits, a measure of how upset she still was.

When Rosetta continued to say nothing, Claire felt obliged to speak. Isaac had been napping but was now stirring and Claire knew her opportunity was limited. Isabel would last awhile. She was sitting on the floor and playing happily with a slinky toy that Claire had brought along. Claire cleared her throat nervously and began.

"I could have lost them—just like that—if you hadn't noticed, Rosetta." There was no response, and Claire went on. "I have a 16-year-old with profound disabilities. She was born like that. We got a second chance when the twins were born and I could have destroyed them, too."

Rosetta nodded her head and finally she spoke. "Did you really destroy your older daughter?"

"I don't know. I had a glass of wine when I was three months pregnant. I couldn't resist. I'm just a glutton."

"You don't look like a glutton. Where's the fat?"

Suddenly, Claire was seeing herself as others saw her, and she changed. Her shoulders straightened, and she placed Isaac gently on the floor beside his sister. She then turned her focus fully on Rosetta. "I'm so sorry," she said. "You're the one who's just experienced a devastating loss."

Rosetta nodded, her faced suddenly suffused by sadness. "It looks like we have great loss in common," she replied.

It was then that Claire realized something. Tia might be socially smoother and more tactful than her, but she would not be able to share her suffering with Rosetta at the same deep level as Claire. Tia had lost her baby and had suffered horribly over this loss. Rosetta had lost her adult daughter and was now going through that same kind of suffering, so they had that in common. But Claire had lived a loss for all of Jessie's 16 years and she was beginning to suspect that Mona had been down a similar road with her own daughter.

"Tell me about Mona," Claire said, her usual impulsivity returning. "What was she like growing up? She didn't seem very happy when we knew her."

Rosetta looked at Claire for a long time without saying anything and Claire was beginning to regret her recent outburst. However, she knew this would be her only opportunity to learn more about Mona's past, so she soldiered on.

"Was it our fault that she left the group? Did she talk to you about it? We've all been feeling so guilty."

"No, it was probably not your fault——and no, Mona did not talk to me about it. She probably knew what I would have said."

Claire carefully said nothing, difficult as that was, and just raised her eyebrows.

"I loved my daughter," Rosetta said, "but many times when she was growing up, I wished that I'd never adopted her. She was always unhappy——and always difficult."

"Why do you think that was?" Claire asked softly.

Again, there was a silence but this time it was as if Rosetta was quietly reflecting, remembering bygone times. Finally, she began to speak. "We got Mona when she was only two days old. We felt very lucky and grateful to get a baby so young, new to the world with nobody else's stamp on her, as it were. We asked all the right questions:  how the pregnancy had gone, if there were any background factors that could be of concern——but we didn't get any answers. The social worker just said that the baby had been thoroughly checked over by the attending physician and he had given her a clean bill of health."

"So what then?" Claire prompted. "What caused her to behave like that?"

Another awkward pause ensued, and then Rosetta blurted out a surprising theory. "I think her mother was a drinker, and that she drank throughout her pregnancy with Mona." Rosetta put her head down at that point and it was clear that she was weeping.

Claire stood up and patted her host gently on the back for a moment. Then she sat down again and said, "I gather you have no way of knowing for sure, but I'd like to tell you one of my experiences dealing with Fetal Alcohol Spectrum Disorder and maybe it will help." Claire held her breath, waiting to see how this remark would be received but then Mona raised her head and looked at her expectantly.

"When my daughter was thirteen, she was transferred into a different school for junior and senior high school students and was obliged to share an assistant with an 11-year old boy who had serious behavior problems. Later, it came out that his mother had consumed alcohol regularly, and often heavily, throughout her pregnancy."

Claire stopped speaking then but after a short pause Rosetta asked, "What kind of behavior problems?"

"This boy could be very charming on the surface, but he had no apparent understanding of or regard for limits. He would often run away or have a temper tantrum for no reason at all that anyone could figure out and his assistant would have to run after him or focus exclusively on controlling his behavior. And to do this she would have to ignore my daughter who has some serious health issues and needs supervision at all times. "

"But didn't the school administration try to help, bring in their specialists to figure out a way to deal with him?"

"They tried but then things happened, and he left the school."

"What do you mean?"

"I don't want to get into it right now. But the point I'm trying to make is that in situations like his——and maybe your daughter's——there doesn't seem to be any real answer. You can only manage the problems, not ever really resolve them. Their basic approaches to issues are not much altered by remediation like if somebody has a reading problem, for example. It's about a whole different way of looking at the world."

Rosetta nodded her head when she heard this, seeming to recognize how well this picture fit her late daughter, and Claire saw the tears in her eyes. "I'm sorry if I upset you," Claire said softly.

"No," Rosetta replied, shaking her head. "You've helped, actually. I feel less guilty now. Sad to say, but I think Tammy is better off without her mother. I'll do my best to raise her right and my other daughter, Jocelyn, has offered her full support and will take over if the day comes that I can no longer cope."

Claire tried not to say it, but she could not help herself. "Do you think Mona drank during her pregnancy?" She tensed, anticipating an angry response from Rosetta.

"No" Rosetta said calmly. "I'm reasonably sure she did not. Her husband didn't drink, and she had no history of drinking that I know of. And we never drank when she was growing up."

"So Tammy should be all right then," Claire replied, with just the faintest hint of a question in her tone.

"I think so. We've already had her checked by Jocelyn's family pediatrician, and he didn't find any problem other than she needs to lose a little weight. And we're working on that."

"Where is she, by the way? Has she been napping all this time?"

"No. Jocelyn took her today to get a vaccination. Her own daughter needed one as well, so it was convenient to take them in at the same time. I'm expecting them all back here soon. I promised to make supper for everyone."

"Well in that case, I think we should be going," Claire replied. She started gathering up the babies and all their supplies and when she was ready to leave, she held out her hand to Rosetta. "I have really enjoyed meeting you, Rosetta, and I'd love it if we could continue our relationship. All the other mothers with babies I know are much younger than me and it would be great to have a friend closer to my age to share this experience with."

Rosetta clasped her hand warmly and replied, "I feel just the same, Claire. Please call me when you feel up to another visit and please tell the group to stop feeling guilty about Mona. I'm pretty sure they could not have said or done anything that would have made a positive difference."

"I will do so," Claire replied, "but as for me, I'm still going to be looking into these murders. Whatever Mona's problems, she didn't deserve to end up like this, nor did her husband."

Rosetta nodded and Claire walked towards the door, but then she turned back. "You know," she said speculatively, "our next mother's meeting is this coming Tuesday. Do you think you'd be up to attending with Tammy and telling the group yourself some of what you told me?"

Rosetta started to shake her head but then seemed to be thinking this invitation over more seriously. "Maybe," she said tentatively. "I'll think about it. Can you call me again in a couple of days?"

"I'll do that," Claire said enthusiastically. And then, in her usual rash manner, she blurted out her most recent thought. "Maybe you could come all the time. Maybe it would be good for you."

"We'll see," Rosetta said sadly, back in the cloud of her grief. "Call me." And with that Claire left.

# - 7 -
## A New Development

Isaac and Isabel were asleep extra early that evening, clearly tired from their day out. Claire decided that more outings like that would make all their lives easier and she called Tia to see if a visit would be possible the next day. She also knew that it was Tia's day off from the hospital since she'd managed to negotiate a four-day work week. That meant it would also be a day off for her neighbour, Amanda Roche, who looked after baby Marion when Tia was at work. Maybe she'd be willing to look after the twins for a few hours so Claire could carry out the next stage of her investigation. As she mulled over this possibility, Claire was at the same time preparing a nice supper for herself and Dan. They would be able to eat in blissful silence this evening since the twins had both dropped off to sleep an hour early because of their eventful day. And Jessie was eating her own supper out on the deck with the help of her assistant.

*If this dish works out, it will be an ideal one to add to Jessie's repertoire and a good contribution to the soup section of my cookbook*, Claire mused as she put together a curried fish soup. Dan approved of the dish and reminded Claire to write it down since she often forgot to do that after creating one of her more successful mixtures. But first, she spent some alone time with Jessie, having bargained with Jessie's assistant to clean up the kitchen while she did so. Claire needed to talk through what she knew so far about the murder, what she'd found out today from Rosetta and what her next steps should be. Jessie was the ideal confidant for this purpose because she just listened. She never acted bored and never interrupted or judged Claire or warned her off some proposed new line of approach.

"I think I need to talk to Stefano Amato's brother next, Jessie. Rosetta told me that he's the principal of a new French Immersion elementary school in Southwest Edmonton, just south of the Henday. It received funding to offer both junior and senior kindergarten classes in French to see if immersion students coming from predominantly English backgrounds can attain earlier and more complete fluency in French that way."

Jessie looked at Claire skeptically, and she took that as a need to explain herself more fully. "Yes, I know that the twins aren't even a year old yet, but it's not uncommon to put children on the waiting list for schools with special offerings even as soon as they are born." Jessie still looked skeptically at Claire, so she went on defensively. "Okay, I know that happens more in places like New York than in Edmonton, but how else am I going to get a chance to talk to him? I'm not a police detective and I can't just waltz in there and start questioning him."

Jessie still didn't look convinced, so Claire continued to explain her strategy. "I'll tell him all about you and the twins and how Dan and I had always wanted French Immersion for our children, but we'd had to forget about that after you were born because it obviously wouldn't have worked in your case. With the twins coming, we thought maybe we could try again, and we didn't want to risk missing out a second time by being late out of the gate getting them enrolled."

As Claire talked to Jessie, she was sitting beside her on the loveseat in the family room, musing about what her next steps would be in chasing down Mona's murderer. She had asked Elsie, Jessie's evening assistant, to place Jessie there, using the floor lift. Jessie and Claire enjoyed these times, cuddling together with a blanket over their knees, Claire talking softly in Jessie's ear so she wouldn't be overheard. Jessie had been the recipient of many secret plans through the years that her father knew nothing about until after the fact.

"I know what you're thinking, Jessie. You're wondering how I plan to move from asking about enrollment to asking about his brother, Stefano, and what enemies he might've had. Well, for your information, I've already figured that out. I'll just casually mention that I happen to know Stefano's mother-in-law, Rosetta, so that's how I know what happened, and I'll offer him my condolences.

"And then what, you ask?

"Okay. At that point he might just stand up and expect me to leave, but I won't. I'll just tell him the truth——that I met Mona and feel very bad over what happened. I'll tell him that I intend to find the murderer and that I've succeeded in that kind of mission before. I'll say that I have a close working relationship with the police and that they sometimes use me as a consultant, and I'll ask him to help by telling me anything that could lead me to his brother's killer."

Jessie still looked doubtful and Claire went on. "Yes, I know that there is one possible snag. He may believe, as the police do, that Mona killed her husband and then herself. But I'm going to tell him what Rosetta said, that Mona wasn't suicidal. Even if she had murdered her husband, she would have tried to make it look like somebody else had done it and not killed herself. The way they were found, it just doesn't add up."

The next morning, after Dan left for the office and Jessie for school, Claire busied herself cleaning up the breakfast dishes and getting the twins all fixed up for their new experience. Amanda was arriving at 9:30 to give Claire a couple of hours' free time.

When Claire had tentatively asked for this favor, she was surprised by Amanda's enthusiastic response. Amanda had replied that she was looking forward to spending this time with Isaac and Isabel and in return she only wanted to be updated on the latest lines of inquiry into the murder of Mona and her husband. This had all been worked out in the phone call Claire had held with her the evening before, conveniently scheduled for when Dan was in the middle of watching a hockey game in the den between the Edmonton Oilers and their arch-rival, the Calgary Flames.

Exactly at 10 a.m., Claire approached the front door of the school and was confronted by a prominent sign reading, "All visitors must report to the school office immediately upon arrival." This sounded ominously formal to her ears and made her quailing stomach quail all the more. Once in the office, she gave her name to the receptionist, whose name was Liz according to her nameplate, and Claire was soon shown into an even larger inner office. In it sat a very large man behind a very large desk, and for a dizzying moment Claire felt like Alice in Wonderland. But then she discretely pinched herself and managed to stutter out her name and business——that is, her ostensible business.

"How old did you say your twins are?" Dr. Marco Amato, according to his nameplate, inquired.

"I didn't," responded Claire. "They will be seven months old next Sunday."

"Well," the principal replied, standing up as he spoke, "I'm afraid you've made a wasted trip. We don't register children on our list until after their third birthday, and even then, there's a process to go through."

"What kind of process?" Claire asked, remaining firmly planted in her chair.

The school principal sat down again with a slight huff. "Our curriculum was designed to meet specific needs. We are offering an enriched learning environment and that's not suitable for all children."

"You advertise yourselves as a bilingual program, not an academic challenge program."

"And so we are——but you see, our approach to bilingualism requires a particular level of ability. We are generally dealing with families where at least one parent does not speak French and the language at home is English. Thus, our students have to make a greater intellectual leap to bridge that divide than is the case with children going to a bilingual program in English and a second language where they are already being exposed to that second language at home."

"It seems to me they would be still leaping, only in terms of learning English rather than the second language."

Marco Amato exuded a combination of exasperation and superiority as he looked down his nose at Claire, appearing to consider how he could gauge his response in terms that she might be capable of understanding. Finally, he replied, speaking slowly, "Well, you see, parents who seek out our program for their children tend to be more, er, higher achievers, and their children tend to be the same. Thus, we can keep our learning standards high, as advertised. We could not do that if we accepted just anyone."

"Hmmm," Claire responded. "But as you said, potential students are tested before admittance, so this is a fair and open process I'm assuming——since you're publicly funded?"

"Of course, of course," he replied. "Come back again when they turn three and we'll see how they're doing and if we think they'll be suitable." He stood up then, signaling an end to the interview, but then he made a fatal mistake in his dealings with Claire. "You do know that twins do not always develop equally. We may be able to accept one of your children but not the other."

"I guess you haven't read some of the latest research, then," Claire replied with some spirit. "While one twin may lag behind the other in certain developmental areas in the early years, they generally catch up in any of those areas relevant to their schooling."

"Well, that may be," Marco replied smoothly. "I can only tell you what our ten-year experience in this school has been, and it's not in line with whatever research you're citing."

"At that point, Claire realized that she'd been sidetracked from her main purpose. This business of twin differences was an emotionally loaded one for her but not one that was relevant to her current purpose. She stood up as if leaving and noted the relieved look on Marco's face. "By the way" she said, "I wanted to offer my condolences on the loss of your brother and sister-in-law. I knew Mona, you see——and I've also met her mother, Rosetta, recently."

"Er, thank you. How did you know Mona?"

"We were in the same mother-child support group——until she stomped out in a snit," Claire responded. "Your poor brother must have had his hands full."

"I suppose," he replied cautiously, standing up once again.

But Claire then sat down and she could almost hear him groaning. "They shouldn't have died that way, been murdered like that——and I plan to find the killer."

Marco raised his eyebrows and looked shocked by this statement. "I believe the police have already figured out who the killer was so I very much doubt that they need your help," he replied with more than a hint of sarcasm in his voice.

"Actually, they do——because they've fingered the wrong person. Mona couldn't have done it because she wouldn't have killed herself. It doesn't fit with who she was, and her own mother agrees with me on that point."

"In any case, it is none of your business, and I'm not in the habit of discussing family issues in a business context. I think you should leave now."

"What you don't know is that I function as a consultant to the police. I've been able to identify the killer in the last seven cases I've worked on with them and they're quite appreciative of my assistance. If you don't believe me, you can telephone Inspector

McCoy," and she flipped one of his business cards onto Dr. Amato's desk. "Don't you want to find out who really killed your brother?"

Claire watched his face carefully as she said this and saw a sudden flash of the misery that underlay the mask he was wearing. He looked at her but said nothing. She spoke then, more softly. "I need to know more about their relationship, their closest contacts, anyone who might have had any reason at all to do this. I know I'm a total stranger and that you must consider the fact that I even raised the subject as extremely inappropriate, particularly at this time. But time is of the essence and I can't find the murderer if I have to wait for some time down the road when you feel up to talking about it."

Marco continued to say nothing, and Claire gently set her own card on his desk and said, "I'd appreciate it if you would call me as soon as you can manage to talk about this. I assure you that the true killer will not be found if the police continue to follow their present narrow line of investigation." With that, she headed for the door but just as she was closing it gently behind her, she heard him say, "Thank you. I may call."

As Claire reached the outer office, another woman rose from her seat with evident impatience and strode towards and past her, obviously heading for Marco's office. Claire turned to the receptionist with her eyebrows raised. "Oh, that's just his wife, Fiona," Liz replied. Claire walked out, wondering if there was any way she could arrange a meeting with the wife to find out her thoughts about Stefano and Mona.

# - 8 -
## Other Directions

It was the following morning and Claire had just been through a restless night——no fault of the twins. It was her mind that wouldn't shut down properly. Too many dead ends in this case; there must be something she was missing.

Claire heard noises from the kitchen and realized that Dan was getting Jessie ready for school. Claire mentally congratulated herself once again on having acquired such a supportive husband, but just then she heard a cry from the twins' room. *They must have slept all this time,* she marveled. *What did I do to deserve that?* Claire quickly hoisted herself out of bed and headed for the babies' room and soon the early morning activities were in full swing in the Marchyshyn household.

Just as she finished nursing Isabel, Claire heard the doorbell and suddenly remembered that today, Wednesday, was her free day. With Dan's agreement, she'd recently arranged for Bethany Brown, a neighbour woman in her mid-fifties, to take over with the twins for six hours every Wednesday so she could have a break. Claire frantically reviewed in her mind how to make the most of this brief span of freedom.

There were only two possible avenues of investigation open to her at present, as far as Claire could see. She could visit Mona's sister-in-law——the impatient-appearing wife of the principal, or she could visit Mona's mother, Rosetta, to try to get more information on the pair of them, or she could do both. Naturally, she opted for the latter route, wanting to move the investigation along as far as possible during this all too rare break time.

Once, Bethany had been oriented to the specific needs of the twins for the day, Claire turned them over to her and quickly made her arrangements. First, she phoned Rosetta to find out Fiona's last name and place of work. Then she looked up the phone number in the on-line Edmonton directory. She phoned and was surprised and pleased to get through directly to Fiona. After hearing the reason for her call, Marco's wife suggested that they have lunch together at a café near her office so they could maximize the interview time.

Although the midday sun was shining brightly, the café itself was quite dark inside, due to the nature of its configuration. It was a long, narrow room with minimal frontage and therefore minimal windows and Claire had to look hard to find the woman she'd seen only briefly the day before. Finally, she spotted her, right at the back in a bench nook with a tall divider between it and the neighbouring bench. On the wall behind her was a large, rather gloomy looking picture of the Italian Alps which appeared to have been painted on a rainy, foggy day to achieve some image the artist had in mind. *Perhaps he was depressed*, Claire thought sourly.

As expected, Fiona was cautious at first, carefully quizzing Claire on the reason for her involvement and her credentials for being involved. After satisfying her on these two issues, Claire proceeded to say defensively that she didn't believe Mona to be the murderer. She expected Fiona to exhibit the same resistance to this suggestion that her husband had, but was surprised when Fiona expressed agreement with her. "Mona could be a real pill and she was certainly exploitative of Stefano, expecting him to do more than his share where the baby was concerned, but I can't imagine her actually killing him. What would be the point when she was clearly so dependent on his help? Besides, she simply didn't have that kind of initiative." Fiona declared.

"Y-e-s," Claire replied slowly. "In the brief time I knew her, I found her to be on the dependent, self-pitying side——not exactly a mover and shaker."

"You could put it that way," Fiona answered, indicating that she didn't agree entirely with this analysis. "I'd say that it was more a case of her being frustrated and depressed. Her husband wasn't exactly the meek, down-trodden soul he portrayed himself to be and, of the two of them, I'd have to say that I liked Mona better."

Claire's ears pricked when she heard this. "What do you mean by that?" she asked.

Fiona looked at her but said nothing. "You realize," Claire went on, "that the police have decided on Mona as the killer and even though she's not here to pay for that crime, that's the legacy she'll be left with——unless I can find out who the real killer was. Do you want that?"

"No," Fiona quietly replied. "However, I'm not sure I want to find the real killer either."

"Now what does that mean?" Claire asked. Fiona didn't respond and started putting her coat on, but Claire just continued to sit there.

"Look," Fiona finally said. "I have to work late tonight——or at least my husband can think so. There's a restaurant called The Pierogi Palace just a couple of blocks from here.

"I know it," Claire replied, recalling the number of times through the years that her Ukrainian husband had dragged her there——his idea of a really good night out.

"I can meet you there at five and we can discuss this further."

Claire thought quickly, wondering how she could work around her domestic duties for the evening and what excuse she could give to Dan without having to admit her involvement in the case. After mentally reviewing her resources she replied, "If you can make it for six, I can do it."

Fiona stood up then. "I'll see you there at six." She walked away briskly without waiting for a response.

It was after one p.m. at this point and Claire decided she'd have to skip the appointment with Rosetta today and try to see her tomorrow. Maybe she could convince her to come over; that would be easier. Also, it would give her the excuse to bake a cake, which she'd been craving lately. As soon as she arrived back home, Claire phoned Rosetta and made the change in arrangements and invited her for lunch at 12:30. She'd meant to make it only coffee but the words just fell out of her mouth and now she wondered how she was going to juggle child care, some emergency housecleaning and lunch preparation the next morning.

Claire made one more important phone call and then hustled into the kitchen. Bethany would be leaving in an hour and Jessie would be arriving home from school soon after. She needed to get supper ready for her family and to organize what the twins would need for the evening, including the preparation of more formula, before three o'clock because after that she'd be fully occupied with child care duties.

At five o'clock, Dan arrived home and Claire waited impatiently for him to join her in the family room for a catch-up, their after work/before dinner ritual. He raised his eyebrows when he entered the room and saw her dressed for an evening out. Claire hastily explained what she wanted to do without explaining exactly why she wanted to do it, and she tried to look as haggard and worn-out as possible while she said it.

"A new acquaintance, you say. Why have I never heard of her before?" Dan asked.

"Tia put me in touch with her and we had lunch today and found we have a lot in common. As you know, I've been trying to work out what I'll do once the twins are old enough to allow me some free time. This woman works for an interior design company and we spent some time discussing recent trends." Most of this was true except for the part about Tia providing the connection; it just wasn't the whole truth. They had in fact talked shop for about ten minutes of the hour they spent together.

"I thought you'd given up on interior design as a career option. Didn't you tell me that when you started up the group home for Roscoe, Bill and Mavis? Didn't you tell me on several occasions how rewarding you found it compared to your previous career?" Dan looked confused and also somewhat annoyed.

Claire wished she hadn't once again found the need to be sneaky with Dan, but the only alternatives would be to openly defy his demand that she not involve herself in any more murders or to abandon her mission to find Mona's killer. Since neither of these choices was acceptable to her, Claire really had no other choice in her mind. Finally, she said, "I know it's a bit unfair to leave you with the children again, but I really feel I have to keep this meeting. If nothing else, perhaps it'll help me to put the idea of interior design as a career direction out of my mind forever."

"Okay," Dan said grudgingly——but in the future could you please check with me before making plans like this? And I have to say, I think you're missing out on the present by mooning away about future career directions all the time.

"We have a lot to be grateful for with Isaac and Isabel. I don't understand why you can't just be satisfied with being their mother for the time being."

*Dan is angry with me for something I'm not even considering,* Claire thought as she drove a little too quickly down the road. *That's what I get for lying. I just get dragged in deeper and deeper.*

Claire tried hard to put her domestic problems out of her head as she approached the restaurant. She was five minutes late, but found Fiona waiting for her and she actually seemed eager to talk. It seemed to Claire that Fiona had been waiting a long time for the chance to safely share her ideas about her late brother-in-law with someone who might be interested. "Stefano was not who his family thought he was——and Mona was not the monster he made her out to be."

"Why do you say that, Fiona? Her own mother told me that Mona had lots of issues and several of their neighbours have reported frequent arguments between them, and how Mona was the one doing most of the shouting."

"Sure. I know that. There were better ways to cope with her philandering husband than by eating herself into a blob and shouting all the time, but I honestly don't think she had them. If I'd been in that situation, I'd have kicked the bum out and sued him for child support, but Mona was… well, she was just Mona."

At that moment, they were interrupted by the waiter who had come to take their order. Fiona asked for their special, pierogi and grilled Ukrainian sausage with pickled beets. Claire knew these dishes only too well and asked instead for a large bowl of borscht, double caraway rye bread and a side salad. Once the order had been given and the waiter had departed, they resumed their conversation.

"Rosetta told me that she suspected Mona had Fetal Alcohol Spectrum Disorder——FAS-D for short. She was adopted, you know."

Fiona raised her eyebrows. "No, I didn't know that——but why would Rosetta think that Mona's birth mother drank?"

"Rosetta and her husband didn't get a full picture from the social worker when they adopted Mona," Claire explained, "even though Rosetta asked all the right questions. She suspects that the worker was under pressure to find an adoptive home for Mona and just did what she thought she had to do. Since the examining pediatrician didn't find any obvious problems, she must have thought Mona would be okay. But according to Rosetta, Mona exhibited a lot of classic behaviors associated with children who have absorbed alcohol into their system while in utero."

"But aren't there also other signs——facial features and such? I never noticed anything unusual about Mona's appearance—— apart from her weight problem, of course."

"Facial signs are not always evident. It depends at what stage in pregnancy the drinking takes place. It might be that the mother resisted drinking for the first few months and then started back up."

"I still don't understand why her adoptive mother would stick a label like that on her just because of her behavior. Lots of people are depressed or unmotivated. We don't say they have fetal alcohol syndrome or whatever you want to call it."

"It's harder to get a clear picture with adults because we all learn to compensate, at least to some extent, for whatever limitations we have during the growing up process. Mona had great difficulties, both academic and social, in school, to the extent that various school counsellors through the years got involved and tried to help her. At least two of them when talking to Rosetta hinted at the presence of FAS-D. Mona had problems with planning, organization, judgment, and impulse control. She had big problems with maintaining attention and concentration and early on was identified with Attention Deficit Disorder. She couldn't follow directions if given more than one at a time and she lashed out with no regard for consequences whenever she got frustrated, and that happened frequently."

"Well, she managed to marry and have a child so she must have been capable of doing some things right."

"Lots of people with FAS-D are married and become parents— —and lots of those people have remained undiagnosed throughout their lives. One could almost say that the condition is endemic in our culture which traditionally has exhibited a high acceptance of social drinking."

"Okay," Fiona replied. "But if Mona had all these judgment and impulse control issues why would you doubt that she murdered her husband and then killed herself?"

"Because she wasn't suicidal, according to her mother.

Because from everything that Mona shared with her mother or sister, it seemed that she was trying to latch onto anyone who could help her cope, like turning to her mother all the time for babysitting help."

"Lots of young mothers do that," Fiona retorted.

"You know what," Claire replied. "We could argue this point all night, but it wouldn't get us anywhere. I'd like to know more about the husband, Stefano. What can you tell me about him?"

"I didn't like him. Everybody seemed to think he was so meek and downtrodden. His family knew about some of his affairs, but they excused that behavior saying that as Mona was such a nag and complainer, he had to find his happiness elsewhere. I never bought it. Mona's mother saw it, too. Mona told me that before they were married, her mother warned her against him, but she didn't listen and married him anyway."

"Can you tell me about any of his behaviors in particular that upset you or that raised a red flag for Rosetta?"

"Well, I don't really know Mona's mother well. I got that information from Mona herself. What I didn't like about him for starters was that he was such a hypocrite. He always pretended to be so modest, but he sneakily took every opportunity to make himself look good, even special. Also, he was very quick to take offence if anybody criticized him for any reason——and he was not emotionally supportive of Mona in any way that I could see. She was really struggling after the baby was born and all he ever said about her——behind her back and to everyone who would listen——is that she was lazy and always looking for an easy way out. Right to her face and in front of others he'd tell her that she was not much of a mother."

"Wow!" was all Claire could say, thinking once again of all the support she got from Dan and how much he appreciated the good things about her. Right then and there she decided to herself that she'd come clean with him about the day's activities and risk the consequences. He didn't deserve to be lied to.

"Also," Fiona went on, clearly on a roll now. "He was never much of a provider, but he made sure to have the best in clothing and shoes for himself. He had his hair cut by a stylist while his wife went around looking like a shaggy dog. Ugh." Fiona finished up in disgust.

As she drove home that evening, Claire was thinking, *What Fiona had to say is very interesting and it puts a whole new perspective on things. Now I need to talk to Rosetta about what she thinks of Fiona and Marco and find out if she agrees with this view of her son-in-law. Then I need to talk to her other daughter and son-in-law to get their points of view on both Mona and Stefano.*

Claire was happy and satisfied with the evening's work and the further lines of enquiry that were now emerging. But then she remembered the other direction she had to pursue and realized she needed to contact Fiona again to see if she had names for her——the names of the other women who'd been a part of Stefano's life. Their husbands would've had a reason to get rid of Stefano——or to make him pay for what he did, even if the affairs were over. *But that would not explain why Mona was killed,* Claire mused. She was the innocent victim of the affairs. Okay, what about the other women? One of them might have really been in love with Stefano and convinced that he felt the same about her. And if he tried to break it off, she might have been angry enough to kill them both.

Claire's head was spinning. *None of this really makes sense,* she thought. *Are there any other possibilities I need to consider; gambling debts or a case of mistaken identity by a professional hit team, for example?* As she entered the driveway to her home, Claire realized sadly that she couldn't be completely honest about this issue with Dan just yet. *But I'll do some digging and maybe in a couple of days I can tell him what's happening. If I've made some real progress, maybe then he'll understand how important it is.*

# - 9 -
## The Best Laid Plans

By the time Claire returned home that evening it was already 9:30, but she went straight to the kitchen and busied herself making a cake. When Dan wandered in for a visit, she informed him that she'd invited Mona's mother for lunch the next day, as she really needed some support at this very sad time in her life. Dan looked at her suspiciously but said nothing, and he went off to watch the remains of a hockey game that one could now entertain oneself with nine months of the year.

After reviewing the contents of the fridge, Claire chose a recipe that would help clear it out: a 9" x 13" Banana Oat Cake from the *Company's Coming Cake Book* that Tia had given her. The recipe read one way, but Claire mentally rewrote it another way in order to accommodate the various shortfalls and excesses she'd discovered in her hunt through the fridge:

She replaced a missing ¼ cup of butter with 2 tablespoon of mayonnaise, reduced a cup of sugar to ¾ cup, substituted a cup of yogurt for ½ cup of sour milk and exchanged a cup of chocolate chips for ¼ cup of Skor toffee bits, all she had. She then added the remaining ingredients, put the batter into a pan, placed it in the preheated oven and hoped for the best.

Claire waited impatiently for the cake to be done. After testing it at 30 minutes, she put it back for the remaining five because it was still underdone. After removing it from the oven, she noted that it had fallen back on itself slightly——but evenly, i.e., no big drop in the middle so that was a good sign. Claire sat drinking her coffee and scanning the newspaper, but after 15 minutes she got up to cut a small corner out of the cake. It was definitely on the moist side but tasted quite delicious. Next time, she would add an extra tablespoon of flour to compensate for the added liquid and that would help to stabilize it.

Claire smiled smugly to herself. It could be considered a success but not all her efforts were. Her constant need to experiment and improvise was just a part of her rebellious nature. She didn't like following orders, not even the orders in a recipe. In fact, as in this case, she sometimes didn't even follow her own orders but second guessed herself. Claire had considered using only one egg and adding two tablespoons of flour to compensate for the extra liquid from the full cup of yogurt, but she then changed her mind. If she'd done that, the cake might not have fallen. Claire's penchant for using up stuff had worked this time but sometimes it back fired and she wasted more than she would have in throwing the leftover item in the garbage. In this case, she'd gotten away with it, however, and now she could stop worrying about that leftover yogurt and odd remnant of margarine and the, lone, overripe banana——and whatever on earth had inspired her to buy Skor toffee bits.

The next day Claire tried to fit in as much housework as she could around the demands of Isaac and Isabel. Now eight months old, they were beginning to interact more with each other and she was delighted to see that Ike was becoming more assertive in his dealings with Izzie and also that he was showing a stronger interest in his various toys and in figuring out how they worked——trying to take the wheels off a dump truck, for example.

As she straightened, mopped and dusted——one eye always on the twins——Claire reviewed what she was going to serve Rosetta for lunch and how she could manage all that while dealing with the twins at the same time. *Keep it simple, stupid*, she reminded herself. Looking through her fridge, she mentally calculated how she could 'use up' stuff while at the same time creating something, tasty, reasonably healthy and visually appealing. This was one of her favorite forms of intellectual exercise.

Claire spotted a package of fettuccine pasta, not quite as fresh as it had been when she'd bought it three days before on impulse. Like a dog chasing its tail, Claire frequently found herself in the position of having perishable food on hand, purchased on a whim with no thought of how it could be used. Though she was well aware of this personal foible, it never stopped her from making the next unnecessary purchase, drawn to it by either its sale price, its novelty value or some vague appeal she couldn't even properly identify.

Claire scanned the fridge and her eyes fell on a jar of black olives. She placed them on the counter, thinking to herself that there were definitely not enough of them in her cuisine, since Dan didn't like them. That led her to a mulling over of the many small sacrifices needed for a successful married life and that in turn caused her to consider how entitled it was to even ruminate over such a petty first world problem. But Ike's sudden scream of anger over his sister's efforts to grab a toy truck away from him brought her back to her domestic reality with a bang.

Claire took the truck gently from Isabel and gave it to Isaac while handing her a favorite doll in return. Isabel was a calm baby, adaptable and easily pleased. Isaac tended to be fussier and to get upset more easily. He now held onto the truck with an almost smug expression on his face while Claire changed him and put him down for a nap with a bottle. Isabel seemed quite content to sit on the floor a while longer, reveling in the fact that she now had all the toys to herself. This gave Claire the opportunity to proceed with preparing the lunch for Rosetta who would be arriving within the hour.

Claire stirred butter and white flour together in a pan over low heat for a couple of minutes to make a roux. She slowly added enough milk to make a sauce and then stirred in a cup of shredded cheese and some salt, white pepper and dry mustard. Meanwhile, she placed a pan of water on the heat. While waiting for it to come to a boil she washed and finely chopped some yellow pepper, celery, green onion and black olives and microwaved them for one minute. When the water was boiling, she added the fresh fettuccine, watching it closely. When it was still slightly undercooked, she added it to the slightly watery sauce and stirred in the vegetables. She then placed her mixture– — 'mixtures' being another one of the things that Dan could not abide——into a greased, 9-inch square glass cake pan. Over the top she sprinkled some panko mixed with more shredded cheese and a generous sprinkling of a garlic bread seasoning mixture from Costco. It had come in a huge bottle and Claire had been somewhat pressed to find ways to use it up in a timely manner. She then placed the dish in a pre-heated, moderately hot oven, knowing that over the next 30 minutes it would brown nicely, and the cheese would melt. The end result would not be watery, and the pasta would be cooked just about right. This was Claire's spontaneous version of what the Italians call a 'pasticcio,' which translates to "hodgepodge" in English.

As Claire cleaned up the resulting mess on the kitchen counter so she would have the space to prepare a quick salad, she regarded the garlic bread seasoning. Now two years old, it was half empty and needed to be transferred to a smaller container, so it would be exposed to less air. Claire did this quickly and efficiently since one of her upper kitchen cupboards was entirely devoted to storing empty jars of different sizes. Claire justified this strange use of precious kitchen storage space, along with her use of the entire freezer unit in her side-by-side fridge-freezer for her herbs and spices collection as follows:

She particularly enjoyed the taste of herbs and spices which for the most part could only realistically be purchased in dried form. However, stored at room temperature, they lost their aroma and thus their flavor in only a few months; hence, the need to buy in small quantities and replace frequently. Claire didn't like this line of reasoning. She liked economy of scale and not having to run out to the store because she suddenly needed to replace a spice or herb and not endure the use of stale condiments. A long time ago, she'd reasoned that if dinosaurs and ancient humans could be preserved in ice for millennia, then spices ought to be able to last in the freezer for at least a decade, and, so far, this thinking had worked for her, more or less.

Just as Claire began to assemble the salad, the doorbell rang. Simultaneously, the oven timer dinged and as Claire looked towards it, she suddenly became aware of something else. The delicious smell of the pasticcio wafting from the oven was now being overlaid with another not so nice smell and a glance towards Isabel, looking very preoccupied, gave her a good idea of what that smell was.

After quickly reviewing her options, Claire turned off the oven and then ran to open the door. She invited Rosetta and Tammy in and immediately excused herself. Scooping Isabel up, she hurried to the bedroom to change her.

When Claire returned with Isabel, she found Rosetta in the process of changing Tammy. After that matter was settled, they put the two girls down on the floor with some toys to get acquainted and Claire quickly finished putting together the salad and placed it and the pasticcio on the table. They settled the two girls in the highchairs, but just as they sat down to eat, Claire heard a wail from the bedroom and rushed to get Isaac who needed changing and feeding. Meanwhile, Rosetta had taken over feeding both girls as well as herself. Claire sat down at the table with Isaac and gave him a bottle with her right hand while trying to feed herself with her left. Finally, all was managed and Claire shooed Rosetta into the living room despite her protestations about doing the dishes. "We need to talk," Claire said, "and that's more important right now." But she then left Rosetta alone with the children and returned five minutes later with cake and coffee.

"I have now met with both Marco and Fiona," she told Rosetta. "Marco wasn't willing to talk to me about the situation, but Fiona told me some interesting things about Stefano, and she doesn't think that Mona is the killer either. She also said that she liked Mona better than Stefano."

Rosetta looked happy when she heard this, and Claire went on. "Fiona's description of Stefano made him sound very cold and self-centered. She knew of several affairs he'd had since his marriage, and she thought that Mona must have known about at least some of them. She saw Mona as kind of weak, low in energy and unhappy, turning to food for comfort. Mona didn't seem to her the kind of person who would murder her husband, no matter how much he might have deserved it."

Rosetta nodded solemnly, and Claire continued to speak. "If Stefano had all these affairs, then I need to talk to the women involved. I need to know if any of their husbands were upset enough to take out Stefano and maybe kill Mona in the process because she was a witness. Do you by any chance know any contact information for any of them?"

"Mona never mentioned anything like that," Rosetta replied. "She complained about Stefano staying at work so long and not helping out much with Tammy when he was at home and never wanting to take her anywhere for an evening out. But she never mentioned any other women."

"Do you think she really didn't know?"

"Well, what I do know is that Mona was really good at denying what she didn't want to accept. So, I suspect that she knew but she didn't know——if you know what I mean."

"A 'stick your head in the sand' kind of person," Claire replied——and Rosetta nodded.

"What about your other daughter? Do you think she might know anything about Stefano's affairs? Do you think Mona might have talked to her?"

"Hard to say. They were never very close. Jocelyn resented

Mona because she took so much time and attention when they were growing up. I think Jocelyn feels that she was short changed." But after a pause, Rosetta went on, "It wouldn't hurt to talk to her, though. They knew some of the same people. Jocelyn might have heard something, or Mona might have told her something that she didn't want to share with me. I know that they phoned each other once in a while although they rarely got together socially as couples or went shopping together or anything. I can give you Jocelyn's phone number. She works fulltime, though. She's a lawyer, you know," Rosetta said proudly. "But maybe you could meet her for lunch sometime."

"That would be great," Claire replied. "When you talk to her would you please tell her I'll be calling and that you really want me to keep looking into this murder?"

"I'll do that," Rosetta promised. "I'll call her this evening. And here is Jocelyn's number," she added, scribbling it down on a corner of her paper napkin and handing it to Claire.

"Thank you," Claire replied, and then added, "What about her husband? Did he ever socialize with Stefano on his own? Would he possibly know some of Stefano's contacts?"

"I doubt it. I know he didn't like him particularly. But you can ask Jocelyn what she thinks."

Claire had to be satisfied with that and indicated that she'd try to get in touch with Jocelyn tomorrow evening and that hopefully Rosetta would've spoken to her by then. After Rosetta left, Claire looked at the dishes but suddenly realized how achingly tired she was. Both children miraculously decided that they needed a nap and Claire lay down with them and promptly fell asleep. And that's the way Dan found them when he came home from work——the three of them sleeping, Jessie now home from school and swinging in her hammock and her new, after school assistant, Marcella, busily cleaning up what appeared to have been a huge mess in the kitchen. Later, Claire told him that she wasn't having any more lunchtime visitors any time soon. With two babies to care for it was just too much.

# - 10 -
## Things Get Interesting!

It was the following afternoon and Claire was only now beginning to recover from her mammoth effort the day before. *Tonight is going to be leftovers*, she said to herself—or maybe steak. Steak sounded good. That way she could justify opening a bottle of red wine. But before devoting any further thought to mundane domestic issues, Claire thought that she had better phone Jocelyn while there was still time to catch her at work.

"Brady and Son Law Office," the receptionist replied coolly. "How may I direct your call?"

"Uh, may I speak to Jocelyn, please?" As usual, Claire was not prepared and replied somewhat ungraciously.

"Ms. de Felice is engaged at present. May I ask who's calling?"

"Um, my name is Claire Burke. I'm a friend of her mother's." Claire gave her number and quickly hung up but within five minutes, Jocelyn called her back. Claire explained the purpose of her call, but Jocelyn didn't sound too enthusiastic about meeting.

"So you actually think your sister is the murderer?" Claire asked, a hint of confrontation in her voice.

"No, it doesn't really sound like something she'd do——something she'd have the gumption to do. She was hardly that much of a mover and shaker."

"Well, then?"

"I don't feel the need to know who murdered her. It's done now. Nothing can change that."

"What about justice? I thought lawyers were supposed to be all about justice."

"Yes…no…look, I'll meet you at Franco's at noon tomorrow. I have a light day and can manage an hour lunch. Do you know where that is?"

"Yes, it's near your office, I believe. I looked it up."

"Oh!" Jocelyn replied, sounding surprised. But she did not say anything further except good-bye.

Claire had difficulty finding a parking space near the restaurant the next day. Also, she'd left late because Dan couldn't take over with the twins, and it was 20 to 12 by the time Amanda Roche had dispatched her other commitments and arrived. Then it took another five minutes to orient her as to what Claire had prepared for their lunch and other matters. Finally, at 12:15, she arrived breathless and apologetic just as a tall, grim-looking woman rose from her chair and headed briskly towards the door. Claire took a chance and intercepted her.

"Are you," she panted and then took a deep breath. "Are you Jocelyn?"

"Yes," the woman replied coldly, looking pointedly at her watch, "but I have other things to do."

"Please!" Claire begged. "You said you had until one. My sitter was late and parking here is impossible——I really need to talk to you!"

Jocelyn hesitated for a moment and then relented. With a cool nod of her head, she headed back to the table she'd just vacated. Claire followed meekly in her wake. They sat down and Jocelyn looked at her mutely.

Claire quickly reviewed everything she'd learned about

Jocelyn and began, "I've met with your mother, twice now——and I really like her. We seem to have a lot in common and enjoy each other's company. Both being older mothers and all." Claire went on defensively when faced with Jocelyn's inscrutable stare and general lack of responsiveness.

"That's nice," Jocelyn said, in what appeared to be a neutral tone but might have been meant sarcastically.

"Well, uh——what I meant was that we've talked quite a lot and I know a bit about what was happening as you were growing up, how difficult and time-consuming Mona was and how that might have affected you."

If Claire thought that that would soften Jocelyn up, she had badly miscalculated. "I fail to see how that's any of your business——or how it has anything whatsoever to do with the question of the murder or——more likely——murder-suicide," Jocelyn said in an angry voice, beginning to get up from the table.

"Please don't leave," Claire begged urgently, in a louder voice than she had intended.

Jocelyn sat down abruptly, obviously not wanting to make a scene. "Keep your voice down," she hissed.

"Look," Claire said, speaking rapidly. "She was difficult, unlikeable——and your childhood would likely have been a whole lot happier if your mother had never adopted her. I get that. But she still didn't deserve to be murdered."

"If she was," Jocelyn sniffed.

"Did you know her husband had several affairs after they were married?"

Jocelyn looked at her, stunned. "No. I didn't know. Mona never said anything."

Claire sat back and observed the rapid exchange of emotions shifting across Jocelyn's face: first surprise, then compassion and finally guilt. *For someone who presents as so cool and collected, she certainly wouldn't make a good poker player,*

Claire thought.

Out loud, she said, "According to her sister-in-law, it was common knowledge in their circle. I'd be surprised if Mona didn't know."

Another minute passed and Claire could see by her face that Jocelyn was rapidly rearranging her thoughts. Finally, she spoke, but what she said wasn't what Claire had expected to hear. "That's why she did it," Jocelyn exclaimed. "That's why she killed him. She'd had enough."

"No, no!" Claire cried out involuntarily. "She couldn't have done that. She was weak. Everybody I've talked to said she was weak. Your own mother says so."

"What do you know? What does anybody know? I'm the one who grew up with her. I know what she was really like. She could turn on you in a flash. Strike like a snake. She didn't care about anybody but herself——least of all me. Everything had to be the best for Mona because she deserved it, or so she thought."

"But that's just it," Claire interjected eagerly. "She didn't think. She couldn't."

"What are you talking about? Mona was a lot of things but stupid she wasn't. Lazy? Yes. Shiftless? Yes. And, as a result she was a total washout at school——but not because she was stupid."

"I am pretty sure from what I've heard that she had Fetal Alcohol Spectrum Disorder. That's why she couldn't make good judgments and why she was always getting into trouble."

Jocelyn stared at her with an incredulous look on her face and then rose to her feet, grabbing her briefcase from the floor with one quick snatch of her hand. "I don't know who you think you are," she hissed. "Who asked you to come around sticking your nose into our family business and making these kinds of wild statements? I've got nothing more to say to you and if you bother me again, I'm going to lay a harassment charge." And with that she strode angrily across the restaurant and out the door before Claire could give her prepared response——"Your mother".

Claire sat there alone a few minutes, trying to quiet her

thoughts, vaguely aware of the curious glances she was receiving from other patrons. She tried to move on in her mind, despite the stinging numbness she was feeling. *Where can I go from here?* she asked herself.

I need to speak to her husband but how can I do that now? She had no answer, and a few minutes later she left the restaurant.

# - 11 -

## When a Door Closes...

The next morning Claire called Rosetta, bracing herself in the event that she got a rather chilly reception if Jocelyn had already called with her version of events. However, Rosetta greeted her warmly.

"Uh," Claire stuttered. "Did Jocelyn call you about our meeting?"

"Y-e-s," Rosetta acknowledged. "She was pretty upset."

"I'm sorry I upset her. I was only ..."

"No need to explain. I know how Jocelyn is."

"Oh," Claire replied, surprised and relieved. Then, with this matter out of the way, she briskly moved on with her own agenda in typical Claire fashion. "The trouble is that I don't know where to go from here. I was hoping to talk to her husband but that seems out of the question now."

"Would you like me to talk to him?" Rosetta asked. "Of course, you'd have to tell me what you want me to say."

"Would you?" Claire breathed. "That would be wonderful.

Please find out how he felt about Mona and whether he knows of any enemies she might have had. Can you do that?"

Rosetta agreed and said she'd try to arrange a lunch meeting that very day.

It was the next morning and Claire went about her daily tasks in a cheerful frame of mind. Jessie had gone off to school and Dan to work that morning with no incidents. The twins were in a happy and peaceful mood so Claire thought she would risk taking them grocery shopping. Once she'd wrestled the somewhat cumbersome double stroller into a folded position, she managed to lift it into the trunk and then set about fastening the twins into their respective car seats at the back of the van. Now nearly ten months old, they were no longer infants and she was feeling safer about having them so far away from her in the van.

Claire's original plan had been to go the nearby No-Frills store but with the twins in such a good mood she thought she might risk a trip to Costco. If Dan had been around, he would have instantly told her that it was an insane idea to attempt a trek around such a huge store with its tempting giant boxes of everything with two babies in tow. But he wasn't there, and Claire thought she could chance it.

Fifteen minutes later, they arrived at the Costco store and Claire parked the van near a cart rack. She retrieved one and carefully loaded Isabel into the front tot seat. Then she placed Isaac in the carrier on her back. After that, she pulled bags out of the trunk and locked the car. Only then did she realize that she was sweating from the exertion and already tired. And she hadn't even started yet.

Once in the store, Isabel looked around with interest and Claire imagined that Isaac was doing the same. She walked leisurely along a couple of aisles, her favorite part of Costco trips, but suddenly she heard a rustling sound behind her. Claire swung around just in time to observe a stack of potato chips falling to the floor. She stooped awkwardly in an attempt to pick them up, but a near-by customer waved her off and did the job herself. "That's a busy little guy you have there," the other woman said. "He was determined to get one of those bags of chips and finally pulled so hard that the whole stack fell down."

Claire thanked her fulsomely and decided that she'd better walk more quickly and stick to the middle of the aisles. But she was secretly pleased at Isaac's show of initiative and fine motor control. *I guess I can stop worrying about his slower development,* she thought happily.

At that moment, she turned a corner and ran directly into Rosetta who was also shopping and also had her grand-daughter, Tammy, in the tot carrier on the cart. The two girls reached for each other and the women laughed.

"I was going to call you," Rosetta said. "I was able to have a late lunch with Jason yesterday because he had some slack time at work and the situation is not at all as you imagined it to be. He doesn't share Jocelyn's opinion of her sister although he's not too impressed by his brother-in-law. And he feels strongly that the killer needs to be found and held to account. He was very happy to hear that you're looking into it and wants to meet with you to see if he can help in any way.

"That's wonderful news!" Claire exclaimed. "When?"

"He suggested that the three of us have lunch tomorrow, but I told him about the babies and that I wasn't sure if you could swing it."

Claire thought for a moment. Dan would be going into his office for the day tomorrow, but it was Wednesday, so Bethany, her once a week helper, would be there. *I could invite Jason and Rosetta and make my nice Chinese tofu and vegetable dish,* Claire thought. But then she straightened her shoulders and shook her head. *No. This is an information gathering meeting, not a social occasion. And with Dan away and Bethany with the twins, I can slip out for a couple of hours and he won't be any the wiser.* Claire conveniently forgot the promise she'd made to herself to no longer hide her sleuthing activities from her husband.

To Rosetta, still waiting for a response, Claire replied, "I can make it if we can choose a restaurant close to my house. That way I can get home quickly if I need to. There's a really nice pizza-pasta place called Pistachio's just two blocks away from where I live. Would that work?" Rosetta agreed, stating that Jason's office was actually not that far away from there.

At 12:05 p.m. on Wednesday, Claire entered the cozy, familiar restaurant——and suddenly remembered that the downside of familiar was that one of the staff might casually mention her visit to Dan if they ran into him. *Oh, well. I'll have to take that chance,* she thought. *How else am I ever going to make any progress on this case, given my domestic circumstances?*

Jason Albright was slightly above average height and a few pounds on the heavier side. His full head of brown hair was just beginning to grey and he had a cheerful, welcoming kind of face. *He would make a good salesman,* Claire thought. Jason greeted her with a pleasant smile, very different from Jocelyn's suspicious expression. Once they'd settled and placed their orders, Claire turned to Jason and said, "You must be wondering why I'm snooping around in your family business?"

"Not at all," Jason replied. "Rosetta told me all about your past crime busting activities, how you two met and why she's agreed to your offer of help. And it's certainly even more her business than mine. She lost a daughter, after all." Rosetta smiled sadly but said nothing.

"Thank you for understanding," Claire said. "But right now, I'm at a dead end, and I really need some help. Do you know any other close contacts of Mona or Stefano who I might be able to talk to?"

Jason thought for a minute. "They talked about the Gordons a couple of times. I think he was a business associate of Stefano—another financial advisor. I forget his first name. Jocelyn might know."

Claire shook her head. "Better not," she said. "Do either of you have access to Mona and Stefano's house? Maybe we could fine a personal phone directory that would have that entry. Maybe even other contacts I could follow up on."

"I do," said Rosetta. "But the police took some stuff away. It might not be there."

"They phoned me at my office yesterday to say they want to return it," Jason said. "I guess they couldn't reach you or Jocelyn. They're closing the file. They feel they have their answer."

Claire could not help sneering at that. "Always so quick to wrap things up neat and tidy, whether they're right or not."

I'll pick the stuff up tomorrow," Jason said firmly. "And before that, I'll ask Jocelyn for the key so I can go to the house to check if anything else is there that could point us in a new direction."

"No," Rosetta said. "It's better if I go with you. Then, if Jocelyn has any objections, I can tell her it was something I needed to do, and I asked you to come along for support."

"How are you going to do all that without Jocelyn finding out?" Claire said. "She won't like it and will want us to stop."

Rosetta started to reply but Jason interrupted. "This is crazy," he said. "I'm just going to tell her." He turned to Rosetta. "Nobody has more need or right to find an answer than you, Rosetta," he said softly. "And the house now belongs to Tammy and you're her guardian and trustee."

"Co-guardian and co-trustee," Rosetta corrected. "Jocelyn has as much authority as I have. That's the way I wanted it … in case something happens to me while Tammy is still a minor."

"Well, then we're back to square one," Claire said, remembering Jocelyn's negative response.

"No," Jason said. "I'm going to talk to her and straighten this out."

The other two looked at him doubtfully. "When Jocelyn sets her mind to …." Rosetta started.

But Jason interrupted again, clearly agitated. "It's my wife you're talking about and——no offense, Rosetta——but at this point I think I know her better than anyone. Yes, she can be stubborn and difficult and come across as cold and suspicious——and I know she's had a lifetime of resentment built up against Mona. But that's not who she really is underneath. All that is just a protective front, and I know that in spite of everything, she loved her sister and right now she's suffering. She's not sleeping well these nights and I hear her crying out at times. I think she's having bad dreams and I've asked her——but of course she won't admit it.

Rosetta looked stricken when she heard this and started to say something but again Jason interrupted her. "Rosetta, I'll get those items from the police tomorrow as soon as I can, and I'll call you if there's a phone book there. We'll leave the house exploration until I have a chance to talk to Jocelyn."

Rosetta nodded and Jason turned to Claire and said almost pleadingly, "Jocelyn is not who you think she is. She's a really good mother and a wonderful wife, and she's helped a lot of people through the years. She cares about others… it's just her way," he ended weakly.

Rosetta had tears in her eyes at this point, but Claire glanced at her watch and stood up.

"Okay, Jason," she said. "I have to go now but I won't do anything more until I hear from you. I can't, anyway. There's nowhere to go."

As Claire drove home, her mind was occupied by her own guilty thoughts about this latest deception with Dan. *Jason is doing the right, the honorable thing in talking openly and directly to Jocelyn,* she thought. Why can't I? But she knew the answer——or thought she did. Jason can impose his will on Jocelyn, and he has the testosterone to back him up. But I can't do that with Dan. Feminism has come a long way, but that ancient male patriarchy is still lurking in the wings. Dan will just say that the children need me, and I have no right to take risks. But if the situation were reversed, he wouldn't feel the same way, even though the children need him just as much as they need me. Hc's a great parent, better than me in a lot of ways, but that wouldn't stop him from doing something he deeply believed in even if a small risk were involved.

Claire felt considerably better after this rumination. She and Dan had a peaceful dinner together with the children, enjoying the meatloaf that Bethany had prepared. And after the children were all tucked into bed, they spent a happy couple of hours watching a Netflix movie called *Feel the Beat*. Claire thought this was a safer form of togetherness than spending too much time discussing their respective days.

# - 12 -

## A Way Forward

Jason called Claire the next evening. Fortunately, it was after the twins were asleep and while Dan was engrossed in a hockey game between the Edmonton Oilers and their arch-rival, the Calgary Flames, so she was free to talk. The police had been in possession of the personal directory which Jason now had, having picked it up that morning. He was able to give her the Gordon's phone number and address as well as their first names——Nell and Gerry. "There were some other possible contacts, too," he went on. "What I did was just photocopy all the pages with entries. There were only eight of them so I cut and pasted them together and they all fit on two pages. I can send them to you if you'll give me your email." Claire agreed and gave him her address.

"Did you talk to Jocelyn yet?" Claire asked.

"Yes, I did, and then Rosetta called and also talked to her. Jocelyn has agreed not to interfere with our sleuthing, but she doesn't want any part of it. She did agree for you to be involved but she keeps wondering why. She thinks you should have your hands full with three children——one disabled and two still infants——and she does wonder why you aren't putting all your energies there."

Claire thought to herself, *I'm never going to like this woman. She has three children herself and she's a big, fancy lawyer. What right has she to question my desire to do something socially useful outside the home?* Aloud, she responded to Jason, "And do you feel the same way?"

"No, I'm really glad you're willing to help, and I admire what you've accomplished in other cases, according to what Rosetta has told me. Lots of crimes go unsolved because nobody cares enough to keep looking for the answer once the police have devoted their allotted slice of time to them."

*Nice role reversal in this family*, Claire thought sourly. *He's the enlightened feminist, and she's the patriarchal type——while neatly excluding herself.* Aloud, she said, "Okay, I'll keep working on this then. I can find the time to seek justice for Mona, but I can't find the time to argue with someone who doesn't feel the same way."

Jason quickly came to Jocelyn's defense, but Claire ended the call as soon as possible, still steaming over what she saw as condescending superiority and covert sexism on Jocelyn's part.

It was three days later before Claire had the opportunity to involve herself further in the case. Jason had made an initial phone call to the Gordons and had spoken to Nell. She'd expressed her commiserations to him and the family once again and agreed to a meeting with Jason and Claire. Rosetta didn't want to participate further now that she knew both Jason and Claire were committed to finding an answer. She found it all too painful.

"I've arranged to meet up with one of the mothers from the group tomorrow evening," Claire lied glibly to Dan. "She asked if she could talk to me privately about some matter. Bethany's going to come and stay until the twins are in bed. Okay?"

"I guess," Dan said grudgingly. "I suppose she wants your help or advice on something. Just remember, Claire. You can't save the world, especially now," he said meaningfully.

"I know," she sighed, a serious look on her face. "But I do like to help where I can. It makes me feel like I'm still in the game."

Dan gave a resigned sigh. "I understand your frustration, Claire——but it won't always be like this."

"I know," she replied. The children were all in bed and Claire walked away then, muttering over her shoulder about a new book she was anxious to read. *After this meeting, I'm definitely going to tell him,* she said to herself, guiltily.

The next evening, Claire and Jason arrived separately but simultaneously at the Gordons' house and were greeted by both the Gordons when they rang the front doorbell together. Gerry was a greying, slightly built man in his late fifties, just below average height and with a serious air about him. But he had a frank and open face with clear grey eyes. Nell was about the same age and almost his height but gently rounded with sparkling blue eyes and a round face suggestive of humor and good nature.

Soon Claire and Jason were comfortably ensconced in the Gordons' living room with a pot of de-caf coffee and some Peek Frean Bourbon Crème cookies in front of them. After Claire had been introduced and some initial pleasantries had been exchanged, Nell was the first to broach the subject. "I thought that the police had concluded that this was a straight-forward case of murder-suicide. Are you thinking that they're wrong?"

"We want to know what you think," Jason replied. "You seem to have been as close to them as anyone outside the family."

Gerry shook his head. "We weren't really all that close. I worked with Stefano and we were invited to their home two or three times, and I think we had them over once, but..." He waved his hands helplessly and Nell took over.

"We didn't really like them, you see," Nell said bluntly. She was obviously the more honest and direct one of the two. "We only invited them back out of obligation and we only accepted their invitations because we couldn't think of any graceful way around it, and Gerry does… did have to work with him."

"Why didn't you like them? Did you get any sense of what their relationship was like? Do you think Mona could have done something like this?" Claire asked, blurting out all her questions at once as was so typically her style.

Nell and Gerry looked at each other and then he spoke. It seemed like Nell and Claire between them had broken the ice and he now felt free to express himself more openly.

"I actually didn't like Stefano all that much and I never felt comfortable talking to him. He would chatter on about sports or some political issue or other, but he was very closed about anything to do with himself or his family. He did drop the odd hint suggesting that he was in a difficult position with a weak, clingy wife, a helpless infant, and being expected to carry more than his share of the load. As a matter of fact, when I think of it now, I'd say he was actually quite disparaging towards Mona even though he portrayed himself as the silent, loyal, long-suffering type."

"It was just little things, little hints we picked up on," Nell added. "He'd roll his eyes at times and get this grim look on his face whenever she said something he disapproved of."

"The way he dressed so stylishly while his wife always looked like she shopped at a charity store whenever I saw her was kind of weird," Gerry added. "You don't usually see that kind of style contrast with couples——one looking exceptionally smart and the other looking dowdy."

Claire didn't respond but just raised her eyebrows and Gerry went on. "And it wasn't just about style. There was also the money he must have had to put out. Once I complimented him about some new shoes he was wearing. I'd seen the same ones in a store window and been struck by them. But they were way out of my budget——over 300 dollars. He looked kind of embarrassed when I mentioned that, and I never saw him wearing them again."

"So what are you really saying here?" Claire asked bluntly.

"Are you thinking that he had some other source of income?"

"It seemed that way," Gerry muttered. "And he was always so secretive. That's why I just didn't feel comfortable around him. He didn't seem real, somehow."

"How did you feel about Mona?" Jason interjected.

Gerry looked towards his wife for help and she jumped in. "We are doers in this family, and she was a whiner. I've never had much patience with that kind of person."

"Well, just a minute," Gerry responded, speaking more slowly and thoughtfully than previously. "I think she had something to complain about. She talked a little bit about her family. It wasn't really appropriate, but it was like she had nobody else to talk to and was kind of desperately searching for somebody who'd understand." He turned to Jason apologetically. "She thought that Jocelyn looked down on her and that Rosetta pitied her but didn't really understand her. And you know how Stefano treated her."

Jason nodded but said nothing, and Claire was the one to respond. "But is that enough reason to kill her husband and herself?"

"Maybe," Nell said musingly.

"You don't really sound convinced, Nell," Claire observed.

Nell glanced sideways towards Jason with an embarrassed expression on her face. "I...she seemed to have such low energy and initiative——it's hard to imagine her taking a big step like that." She looked towards her husband for support and he nodded his agreement.

Jason spoke up at this point. It sounds like we all agree that the scenario the police have settled on is kind of unlikely, so what are the alternatives? Who could have killed them? Who could have had a reason to do something like that?"

Gerry looked like he was pondering something and finally he spoke. "I keep going back to how shifty Stefano was. "Once he started to say something to me about 'a great deal'——and then he stopped suddenly. When I asked him what it was about, he just said something to the effect that I wouldn't be interested, and then he changed the subject."

"What could that mean?" Jason asked. "You're both financial advisors. Do you think he was into insider trading?"

"Very unlikely," Gerry replied. "We're closely monitored and regularly audited. And we have all been warned how steep the penalties would be if we ever tried something like that."

"Maybe he had gang connections? He does have an Italian name after all," Nell suggested.

Jason bristled at this. "There's nobody in Mona's and Jocelyn's family involved with the mafia. Besides, they're from the North——much less likely there."

"But Stefano…" Nell started but Claire quickly cut her off and changed the subject, sensing the tension in the air. She knew from Tia what a delicate topic this was for a lot of Italians. "What about Mona? Could she have had any enemies?" she asked.

"I never heard her talk about anybody likely to kill her. She mentioned a couple of girls at school who really had it in for her——but that was years ago."

"I gathered together a list of names and contact information that I found in Stefano and Mona's family phone directory," Jason said. He pulled out copies and handed one to each of the Gordons. Do you recognize any of those entries?"

"The entry for us has our old address and we moved two years ago. Is it possible that they have a new directory?" Nell asked.

"I didn't get any others back in the pile of stuff the police took. Mona was pretty overwhelmed with the baby so she might have just neglected to make the address change. And it wasn't the kind of thing Stefano would do. He'd have seen something like that as Mona's job," Jason replied.

Gerry was studying the list of names carefully and now he spoke up. "This entry for Ian Turner? I pick up the phone for our office receptionist sometimes when she's on a break. An Ian Turner called one day for Stefano and he sounded kind of irate, threatening even."

"What do you mean 'threatening'? What did he say?" Claire asked.

"Stefano happened to be out, and I told this Turner guy so. And he said something like, 'Well, you tell him he better phone me——or else."

Claire and Jason looked at each other. She could read what he was asking of her. "I can't do it. I can't call him," she said. "First of all, I wouldn't have any legitimate reason to do so. Far better coming from you. Secondly, I promised Dan that I wouldn't involve myself in any more potentially risky situations."

Jason looked downcast and Claire remembered that he hadn't been honing his sleuthing skills for a number of years like she had. "Look," she said. "You just call as a member of Stefano's family and tell him that the family's very upset and wants answers. His name was in the book and you're just calling everybody there to see if anyone has any knowledge of Stefano's affairs that could help. You don't accuse him of anything or even hint at it. You just kind of ask questions around it, like 'How did you know Stefano?' and 'Do you know others who might have information on what he was up to outside of work?' Just simple questions like that——and you listen hard for any hesitations or overly glib answers, anything that could be suspicious".

Jason looked at her blankly and finally Claire said 'Okay. I'll call him. But I'm going to have to give him your number in case he wants to verify that I have permission to be involved."

*So much for my idea of going home and telling everything to Dan and hoping to get him onside*, she thought. But I'll use my cell phone and I'll call from some place far away from my house so this person can't possibly get my address.

Nell spoke up then. "There's an entry here for a 'Sadie' with no last name. Mona mentioned that name once when we were together for dinner. It sounded like she was a friend from school who Mona had kept in touch with. "I'd be willing to call her if you like, Jason. Like I said, I did not especially like your sister-in-law, but she didn't deserve to die like that. Nell looked at Claire then, a bit shyly. "I don't have much to do these days so if you need help in other ways or if you'd like my company when you're tracking down a lead, I'd be happy to assist."

Claire thought for a minute before responding. "Usually, I work with my good friend, Tia. But she's very busy raising her two children, helping out with her disabled mother when needed and working full time, so she's less and less available." Turning to Jason, she said sarcastically. "She's the kind of person your wife would appreciate. She has her priorities straight."

Jason grinned at her apologetically and Claire addressed Nell again. "If I get into this any deeper——and I will if that's what it takes to find the answer——I'm going to need back-up. But you have to have a cool head and be able to respond quickly sometimes, and it helps to have a good set of running shoes—— and know how to use them."

Gerry had a puzzled and slightly apprehensive look on his face, but Claire also discerned in his expression the presence of a certain eagerness to get involved himself. Nell had seen it, too, and she turned to him. "Not you, Gerry. You wouldn't be able to be like that, like what Claire needs. But you can be my back-up. I'll let you know where we're going and when to expect us back and whatever contact information we have in advance in case I don't turn up or contact you by an agreed upon time. Okay? And I'll tell you all about whatever happened afterward, but you'll have to keep it all very confidential. Right, Claire?"

Claire grinned. "Sounds like you got the right idea, Nell. I think it might work." *Tia's not going to like it,* she thought. But it serves her right for being so conventional and such a slavishly good wife to that Jimmy.

Claire and Jimmy had been involved in a power struggle as to who came first in Tia's life since Tia had married him, but after little Marion was born Claire had had to back off and accept whatever leftover crumbs of Tia's attention and assistance she could glean. Although rationally she understood that this was how it should be, it still bothered her at some level. Jimmy, on the other hand, clearly resented any time Tia took away from him to spend with Claire and he became absolutely livid on those occasions when he found out that some of that time was devoted to their occasionally dangerous sleuthing adventures. He considered Claire to be 'a bad influence' on Tia and had said so on more than one occasion.

Jason interrupted Claire's ruminations with a further question. "What about the rest of the list? How are we going to handle that?"

Claire and Nell looked at each other and then Claire spoke. "You're going to have to call them, Jason. You simply say that the family is looking for the real answer to these murders since the police seem to have given up, and that you have some friends assisting you. The task you were assigned was to make contact with the folks in the directory. You ask how they knew Mona and Stefano or both of them and if we can arrange to meet with them to discuss the matter further. You stress how important it is to you and how upset Mona's mother is by the false conclusion reached by the police."

"I'll try," he said weakly. He seemed to be one of those people who liked the idea of a cause as long as others did the work or led the way and Claire could understand why he'd have been attracted to a take-charge person like Jocelyn who had definite views on everything.

"This week," Claire stressed. "The trail is already cold and there's no time to waste. We should meet next week at this time to discuss results." She turned to Nell. "Could we meet here? It's safer than meeting in some public place and I can't do it at my home and Jocelyn isn't exactly thrilled by this whole idea."

Nell raised her eyebrows inquiringly at that last remark but nothing more was said by either Jason or Claire. "Of course, you can," she said graciously, "and Gerry can sit in if he wants, right?"

"I see no reason why not," Jason said cautiously. "As long as we all understand the need for confidentiality." He turned to Gerry. "You must be careful not to mention any of this at work just in case somebody there was involved that you don't know of."

Claire chimed in her agreement and Gerry nodded his head. "Of course," he replied.

Claire and Jason left together and expressed their satisfaction with the meeting on the way to their respective cars. "I'll start calling tomorrow," Jason promised. "At work——away from Jocelyn's ears."

# - 13 -

## A Picture Begins to Form

The next morning, Nell Gordon woke up with more enthusiasm for the day ahead than she'd felt for quite a while. Her life had been feeling rather empty recently. The Gordon's two adult children and their families lived too far away for regular contact and while she did visit them from time to time, she often had to go alone. Gerry was still fully occupied with his job and could rarely take the time to accompany her and she didn't like to leave him alone for too long.

It's not that she depended on her children to fill up her life. Until a few months ago, she'd been very busy managing a popular clothing store, part of a larger chain. But then the decision was made to close it as part of a downsizing strategy. Nell had been given a healthy payout and with the pension she'd accumulated it had not had much impact on their family finances. But it had left a large hole in her life.

When Nell had made her offer to assist Claire the night before, she'd read the mixed feelings on her husband's face. She saw there the fear that she might be getting into something dangerous but also the hope that this would help to keep her active mind engaged and bring interest and purpose back into her life. Nell smiled fondly over the memory of that look and thanked her lucky stars once again that she'd found such a good man to share her life with.

After breakfast and a bit of morning housework, she sat down at the phone and called the number listed for Sadie. After three rings, a sleepy voice responded, "Uhh——hullo, who's this?"

"I'm sorry if I disturbed you," Nell said, apologetically. "My name is Nell Gordon and I was a friend of Mona Amato. I..."

"Oh. Mona. I read about that in the paper. I'm so sorry about what happened to her. But ...?"

"I know. Why am I calling you? Her family doesn't believe the conclusion the police have come to. A group of us is trying to find the real answer."

"Oh, good. I agree. Mona could not have done something like that. I've been trying to decide what to do, who to contact. I knew her mother once. Mona and I were in school together. But I haven't talked to her much since then. I didn't know if it was right for me to call Mrs. de Felice or not. How is she? Can you tell me anything more?"

"Yes, but not over the phone. And we need to talk to you, to find out if Mona ever mentioned anything to you that could point us in the right direction to find her killer. Have you had any recent contact with her, say in the last year or two?"

"Yes. I saw her a couple of months ago. We spent an evening together catching up."

"Great. When can we get together?" Nell asked briskly.

"I'm free until about five this afternoon if you want to come over here," Sadie replied. I have the late shift at Cosmos this week, six until midnight. Do you know it? It's a restaurant/bar combo on Whyte Avenue East."

"I've heard of it, but I haven't been there. Whyte Avenue has changed a lot in the past few years. It's really getting built up." Nell paused to think for a minute and then went on, "As for today, I need to contact my associate, Claire Burke, to see if she's available. We need to interview you together, so we don't miss anything. Can I phone you back in a few minutes?"

"Sure"

"Where are you located by the way?"

"I'm on the north side——12307 123rd street. It's a two-story apartment building and I'm in Suite 3. You have to take the stairs. Is that okay?"

"I think it'll be fine. I'll call you right back. Bye."

Nell made the call and Claire was able to make the necessary babysitting arrangements so that by two that afternoon they were sitting on a faded pink sofa in Sadie's suite. Sadie sat across from them; her luxuriant, black hair bushed out on all sides around her small face. She was reminiscing about her school relationship with Mona.

"That girl had a lot of trouble paying attention and following the rules. If she wasn't in detention or in the principal's office, it was probably because she'd skipped school that day."

"How did you become friends?" Claire asked.

"Oh, one day I forgot my lunch and she shared hers with me. She was always generous like that. A lot of the other girls didn't like her, but I thought she was all right."

"Did she ever get into fights or steal things?" Claire asked, pursuing her unspoken theory that Mona was a victim of FAS-D (Fetal Alcohol Spectrum Disorder).

"Mona didn't like to fight, and she avoided confrontations whenever she could. She didn't steal either, at first. But then later on when we got to high school, she did."

"Did she ever get caught?" Nell asked.

"Yes, a few times. She got banned from a couple of stores for shoplifting and once she even had to go to juvenile court. She got a suspended sentence, though, so she was lucky."

"Did you ever see her get really violent, though——maybe if some other kid was bothering her too much?"

"No, not really. She'd lash out if other kids were bugging her, even blackened one girl's eye once, but I personally think she had it coming. That Jennie was a nasty piece of work."

"What about your more recent relationship? How often have you seen her since you both left school?"

"Oh, maybe a couple of times a year. We were both busy with work and dating. Then she married that Stefano guy and she really thought she'd lucked out. He had money and they got a nice place to live, and he treated her good——at first."

"What do you mean, 'at first?'" Nell asked.

"Well, she never really said anything, but I could tell, the last few times I talked to her, that she wasn't as happy as she used to be. I thought it was the baby. She was always complaining about how much work a baby was. But then, a couple of times when I phoned her, I heard Stefano yelling at her in the background and could tell she was embarrassed and then she'd make some excuse and hang up the phone quickly."

"Did she ever make any real enemies, or did she tell you of anyone stalking her or threatening her in any way?" Claire asked, changing the subject too soon for Nell's liking.

"No … maybe. This guy she was dating when she met Stefano was pretty upset when she broke it off with him. He used to phone her and try to wheedle her into meeting up with him. Also, she saw him driving by her house a few times. And once she even caught him looking in the window."

"Did she ever report him to the police?" Nell asked.

"No. She didn't want them coming to the door and upsetting Stefano. She tried to keep the whole thing from him."

"And did she succeed?" Claire asked.

"Pretty well. Mona could be real sneaky when she wanted to be."

"Did she mention any recent incidents, in the last few months say?" Nell queried.

"Not that I can recall. Of course, we haven't been talking much. She's been too busy with the baby. So, there could have been some. I just don't know."

"Last question," Claire said. "Do you think Mona could have killed her husband and herself, leaving a small baby behind?"

"No, but not so much about the baby. It was just that Mona wasn't really the violent type. She was actually kind of a wuss, kind of on the whiney, helpless side, if you know what I mean."

"I think I do, from what I knew of her," Nell agreed.

"Me, too," Claire added. "And that's why we're here. She may have been a whiner and she may have been weak, but she didn't deserve to die like that——and she certainly doesn't deserve to get blamed for it."

"You're right——and I'm glad you're doing what you're doing. Would you let me know what happens, if you find the killer?"

"We'll do that," Nell said, rising. "And thank you. We feel more certain now that we're on the right track." Nell looked toward Claire for approval and Claire nodded.

"Oh," Claire exclaimed, just as they reached the door. "Do you happen to remember the name of this man who was after Mona?"

"Uh…it was Leonard——Len Reicher."

"Great," Claire responded enthusiastically. "What about contact information: phone, address, place of work?"

"No, none of that——except I remember that he worked part-time in a bicycle shop with a funny name: B, Bii——Bif's Bicycle Shop. That was it."

"Excellent. We'll track him down. And Sadie?"

"Yes?"

"Remember. Two people have been killed. And you live here alone. I advise you to not let on to anyone that you're the least bit interested in this matter and certainly don't let on that you have any special knowledge. It could be very dangerous, and you'd never know in time to protect yourself."

Sadie shivered, and then agreed wholeheartedly with Claire's advice.

After they left, Nell looked at her questioningly.

"I've learned that lesson the hard way," Claire replied to Nell's unspoken question. "You be careful, too. Very careful."

# - 14 -

## A New Recruit

Claire had praised Nell fulsomely for her able assistance during the interview with Sadie and she could see how much this had pleased her. She suspected that Nell's recent life had been a little on the empty side, but they weren't well enough acquainted yet to exchange personal details. Instead they'd had the following conversation:"

"What should we do next?" Nell had asked Claire. "That Ian Turner who was on the list? I think he's the most likely contact."

"Hmm," Claire said. "I agree, only it's kind of awkward to call him out of the blue when we have no direct connection with the family. Maybe we should phone Jason first to see if he's found out anything more about him?"

"Or Gerry," Nell suggested. "After all, the call came into his office."

"Maybe," Claire replied uncertainly. "But I think we should call Jason first. And we can also update him on our interview with Sadie."

Claire handed Nell one of her wireless house phones and used the second one to call Jason's office. He answered promptly.

"Are you very busy right now, Jason? Do you have a few minutes so we can update you on our interview with Sadie and find out a little more about this Ian Turner guy before we make the call to him?"

"I have a meeting in 20 minutes, but I can spare a few minutes now."

"Good." After providing a quick recap of their meeting with Sadie, she asked if he'd learned any more about Ian Turner.

"No, and I really don't know about finding out more. Why don't you get Gerry to do it? He works with him, after all." Claire said nothing and the ensuing silence grew a bit awkward. "What I could do if you like," Jason offered, "is to try to track down that former boyfriend of Mona's. What was his name … Len?"

"Leonard Reicher——and he works or worked at Bif's Bicycle Shop."

"Great. Should I do that, then?"

"Fine," Claire responded. "Thanks. And I guess we'll follow up on this Ian character. Bye for now. I'll let you get back to work."

"Good-bye," Nell chimed in from the extension, and they ended the call.

"Well?" Claire asked her, looking a little frustrated.

"It's good that he's going to follow up on Leonard, isn't it?"

"Yeah. Shouldn't be any risk there," Claire responded with a faint sneer in her voice.

"What about Gerry following up with this Ian guy?"

"That's just it," Claire replied morosely. "That is risky. If by any chance Ian's the killer, he'd know exactly where to find Gerry."

"Okay," Nell replied. "But what if he doesn't call Ian right now but he starts by making some inquiries in the office without Ian ever having to know? In any detective story I've ever watched, the police start with every possible suspect and then work to eliminate as many as they can from their inquiry."

"Hmm. But like I said before, there might be something going on in that office that we don't know about and the wrong person might get wind that he's nosing around. Is there anybody there he feels he can fully trust?"

"He's pretty close to the receptionist."

"A lot of things are kept away from support staff. But on the other hand, she's likely to know a little about everybody who works there and could've heard some relevant office gossip during coffee breaks or something. But didn't I hear you say to Gerry that he shouldn't get involved in this kind of activity because he didn't have the right personality for it?"

"I don't know why I said that. If anything, he's a lot more cautious and less likely to speak without thinking than I am. I think I was just picking up on your resistance to involving too many people in the investigation."

"You're very perceptive," Claire said quietly. That's a good skill to have in this kind of work——which really can get dangerous at times."

"Are you going to call Gerry then?"

"Yes, I think so. Shall we do it now?"

"Why not?"

As it turned out, Gerry sounded quite pleased and happy about being included as an active member in their investigatory work. Claire made several suggestions as to how he could best proceed and waited patiently as he wrote each one down. When they finished the call, she was feeling better and realized that this was probably the best approach they could take to this rather sticky issue.

# - 15 -

## The Situation Heats Up

Gerry sat back and thought hard after Claire's phone call. Because of his mild manner, people often underestimated him but he was actually quite shrewd and observant. He'd quickly grasped how dangerous snooping around could be in this case and he sat calculating how to proceed and whom to trust. Nobody, he concluded, so paperwork was the best place to start.

*In one way it was fortunate,* he thought, *that the coroner's verdict on the deaths of Stefano and Mona had been murder-suicide.* Since this tragedy had been determined to be domestic, there'd been no reason for the police to examine Stefano's office. Thus, it remained virtually as he'd left it, except for the removal of a few of his active files that required immediate attention. These cases were then reassigned to the remaining financial advisors on a rotating basis so that nobody was overloaded. Any previous client of Stefano's who called in wishing to review their portfolio, was also reassigned in this manner. Stefano's office was locked, of course, but Gerry knew where the master key was.

The following evening after supper and a few minutes' conversation over their after-dinner coffee, Gerry informed Nell that he had to meet a client who could only see him after hours and who had some questions about his portfolio. "It sounds complicated," he told Nell, "so I'll likely be quite late. Don't wait up for me."

"I hope you can sleep in in the morning then," Nell said fussily.

"Don't worry. I won't go in until eleven so I can have a nice lie-in. I have a light day tomorrow anyway——only a couple of afternoon appointments." Nell smiled, he kissed her goodbye, and he left with only a small pang of guilt for having lied to her.

Gerry was very popular with his clients and received frequent referrals, so his caseload was quite heavy. As a result, he did find it necessary to return to the office for further work from time to time and his presence would not be seen as unusual to cleaning or security staff, the only people likely to be around at night. He parked his car on a back street about a block away, and then walked down the alley behind the building, quietly letting himself in the back entrance and climbing the stairs to the third floor where his accounting firm had its offices. After buzzing himself in, he went directly to his own office and sat down. He observed that his waste basket was empty and there were signs that the rug had been recently vacuumed so the cleaning staff had come and gone but might still be active in other rooms.

After hearing no sounds for ten minutes, Gerry quietly exited his office and, using the master key he'd retrieved from a cubby hole inside the receptionist's desk, he entered Stefano's office which was conveniently next door to his own.

After stepping inside, Gerry pulled a pair of thin cotton gloves from his pocket. These had been a souvenir gift from a high school friend who'd become the curator of a small but prestigious museum. The room was in darkness and from another pocket he pulled out a small pen light. Aiming it at the floor, he rotated it in a slow circle and saw a dark, well-used sweater draped across the back of the desk chair. He grabbed the sweater and, after first using it to carefully wipe the inside doorknob, he arranged it along the floor below the door, packing it in as tightly as possible. Then he turned on the light. If anyone entered the main office, they wouldn't see it shining through and if it was observed from outside it could easily be explained later as his own. From street level it would be hard to distinguish between the two rooms.

Gerry wasn't sure what he was looking for, but he soon found the keys to the two locked cabinets in the room conveniently placed in cubby holes in the shallow desk drawer above the knee hole of the desk. The larger cabinet held the usual assortment of investment portfolios of various clients. Gerry scanned a half dozen at random and because of his own expertise in such matters, he was able to quickly discern that there was nothing out of the ordinary about them. In a couple of cases he thought he might have been able to provide more fruitful advice on some investments but being unimaginative or slightly out of date was not a crime and it wasn't what he was searching for. Finally, he pulled the investment portfolio for Ian Turner but only gave it a brief scan and then placed it in the briefcase he'd brought with him. Time was of the essence and he couldn't expect his luck to hold forever.

After relocking the cabinet, Gerry turned his attention to the smaller cabinet, and it opened easily with the second key he'd found. He soon discovered that this was the home of the accounting files, the second part of Stefano's business. He tried scanning some of these files but found it to be slow work. He didn't have accounting expertise and also, he'd have to compare the expenses listed in each file with the supporting documents that accompanied them.

Just then, he heard the noise of the outer door opening and froze. The heavy steps of the security guard moved slowly down the hall, trying each door as he went. The offices were arranged in a square with hallways on four sides. The guard traversed them and then started again. This time he rattled the handle on Gerry's office door vigorously and called out: "Mr. Gordon, are you in there? I can see the light under your door. Is something wrong?" There was, of course, no answer and, by holding his ear flat against Stefano's door, Gerry could just hear him muttering to himself: "He must have left without turning out the lights."

Soon there was silence again and Gerry heard the outer door closing. He sat for a long time waiting for his heart rate to slow and cursing himself for not remembering to turn out his light. He'd have to hurry now because when the security guard left for the evening, he might look up at the building and see that the lights were on in both offices. Then he'd know that something was wrong. *This is definitely a young person's game,* he thought to himself. He forced himself to continue and carried on with his original plan, hastily selecting three other recent files and their supporting documents and placing them in his briefcase. He couldn't make much out of these files, but he had a very clever accountant friend who'd find something there if it was to be found.

Gerry took one more look around the office but saw nothing else of interest. He turned out the lights and with the aid of his penlight replaced the sweater where he'd found it. Then he left the office, making sure that the door locked behind him. He could hear the guard's footsteps as he patrolled the floor above, so he walked quickly and quietly down the steps and out the back door, resetting the security code as he left.

Only when he was back in his car and had started the engine was Gerry able to breathe properly again. But as he drove down the street, passing the alley behind the building, he could see the security officer's car just pulling out of the building parking lot. If he'd parked in that lot, as he'd originally planned, the guard would've seen his car and recognized it. *You must need a very strong ticker to be a spy,* Gerry thought, as his own heart started racing again.

When Gerry was finally safely back home, he quickly changed

into his pajamas and crawled into bed. "Is that you, Gerry?" Nell murmured drowsily. "I'm here, Nell. Go back to sleep." She snuggled against him and soon he could hear the soft sounds of her sleeping breath. But Gerry lay awake a long time, vowing that he'd never do anything like that again.

# - 16 -

## Finally, a Possible Connection

It was a week later when the group met again at the Gordons', and all that time Gerry had remained silent. Claire had called him once but all he said was that he was still working on it and should be ready to share his findings at the meeting. The day after his adventure he'd contacted his accountant friend, Bill Norton and Bill had agreed to check over the files. Fortunately, his business was in a slow period, which happened sometimes, so he had the time to do it quickly.

At the meeting, Jason asked to speak first, just in case he had to leave early as Jocelyn had some errands that she wanted him to take care of later that afternoon and he'd need to pick up their children from school and daycare.

"I called the names on the list and got through to all but two" Jason began. "After several tries, I finally got an answer on one of the two numbers, but the person didn't know anything about a 'Joel Cowan'. She and her husband had only moved into the city a couple of months previously and this was the number they were assigned. I guess this Joel person either died or left the city or cancelled his phone service for some reason, and then it was reassigned."

"Did you try entering his name in the reverse directory on line? He might have another land line or a cell phone number," Claire suggested.

"No, but I'll do that."

"Or you could try one of the specialized directories. There might be a charge, but I think most of those services will give you a week's free trial."

"I wouldn't mind paying for that kind of service if the cost is reasonable." Jason replied. "I could use it in my business."

"What is your business, Jason?" Nell asked.

Jason flushed and said, "I'm the manager of the sporting goods section in the Canadian Tire Store on Calgary Trail South. But I also run a small tech support company on the side and some of my customers are pretty itinerant."

"Meaning they sometimes disappear without paying their bill?" Claire suggested.

"That's about it. Anyway, I'll get on to this directory and report back on these two individuals next week."

"I'd also suggest that you check the obituaries site for Edmonton and see if either of them turns up there," Gerry offered.

"I'll do that, too. Meanwhile, of those I did contact, I asked all your questions, Claire: how they knew Stefano and Mona, how well they knew them and how long, if Stefano and Mona were also listed in their personal directory, when was the last time they communicated, if they'd ever had a disagreement with either of them and if so how serious, and finally, if they had any mutual contacts who might've had a grudge against them. And I listened for all the signs you suggested: if they hesitated before answering, if they got defensive or answered questions I hadn't even asked, if they were in a hurry to get off the phone without a specific reason or for what sounded like a made up reason, if they sounded agitated or upset that I'd called them on this matter and in general if they didn't sound natural in their responses." Jason had his typed list in front of him and was reading it as he talked. "I think I can fairly say that of all of them I managed to reach, only two left me with any suspicions at all."

"Tell us about them," Nell said.

"Well, first there was the Cyber family. "I talked to Sid Cyber on the phone. His wife was out shopping, apparently and his kids are three and six so there didn't seem any point in talking to them. "

"What made you suspicious about him?" Claire asked.

"His name for one thing. It sounded made-up to me. And when I asked him why his number was in the family directory, he said he knew Stefano, but when I asked him how and for how long, he got very vague. He just said something like, 'Oh, I've seen him around, at bars and such.' I responded to that by saying, 'I didn't know Stefano was in the habit of going to bars. Was this after work or on the weekends?' He said, 'Uh' and there was a distinct hesitation, and then he said, 'After work.' Then I said, 'Oh, do you work near each other?' and he said, 'Uh,' and again there was a hesitation, and then he said, 'I guess so.'"

"It does sound a little off," Gerry responded. "What happened next?"

"I got impatient and said something like, 'Your answers aren't very forthcoming. Is there something about this relationship you're not telling me?' Then he got kind of angry and said that he wasn't interested in playing this cat and mouse game any longer and he didn't know what right I had to phone him and harass him about his relationship with a deceased friend. He wanted to end the call and I quickly said, 'You're quite right. It shouldn't be up to me to ask you these kinds of questions. I'll just pass your name onto the police and leave them to do the job they're paid to do.'"

"Oh, boy. What then?" Nell asked.

"Nothing. I just slammed the phone down."

Claire and Nell briefly looked at each other but said nothing further on the subject of the Cyber family. Claire's private thought was, *Now I know why Inspector McCoy used to get so angry when I got to a witness before he did.* Out loud, she said, "Tell us about the other suspicious contact."

"That was Sheila Hermann——Miss Sheila Hermann, as she told me quite clearly."

"What put you off about her?" Nell asked.

"She talked kind of prissy like——said she was a librarian and she knew Mona because Mona used to come into the library quite often——a few years ago, before she got married and moved out of the neighbourhood."

Claire raised her eyebrows. "Did you ask her when she last talked to Mona?"

"She said, 'A couple of months ago'. She said that Mona just phoned her out of the blue one day. She asked how Sheila was and talked about getting together."

"That can happen," Nell pointed out. "It's happened to me."

"Okay——but when I asked this Sheila if she'd heard about the murders, she said that she'd read about them, but she didn't express any feeling or particular interest. Oh, she did add that she couldn't see Mona as a murderer. 'Not exactly the feisty type' were her exact words, I believe."

"Okay," Claire said. "Well, good. Thanks for doing all that work. And if you can keep digging for those other two contacts that would be great. And I hope you won't be offended if Nell and I call a couple of these people back. It's often good to get different perspectives on an involved party."

Jason nodded and smiled, and then Claire asked Gerry if he'd like to go next. Gerry started by reviewing his late-night adventure with appreciative gasps from the other three.

"Wow, you're a cool one," Jason said, admiringly.

Gerry gave a half grin and then went on to discuss his friend's work. "Bill has actually done some forensic auditing, so he really knows what to look for," he stated.

"But did he find anything?" Nell asked.

"Yes and no," Gerry responded. "Most of the files were okay

except he had the same thought about Stefano's tax accounting work that I had over his financial investment stuff. It was a little carelessly done and Stefano had missed some possibly tax-deductible items, according to the accompanying documentation. But on Ian Turner's file, Bill did find a significant issue."

Gerry paused here and Nell asked impatiently, "What?"

"Ian has some rental property and Stefano had included on his list of deductions an almost $3000.00 claim for a new furnace from a company that does not appear to exist."

"Maybe it's recently gone out of business," Jason suggested.

"I don't think so," Gerry replied. "Bill says he checked thoroughly on the internet and he's sure there would've been some evidence of its existence somewhere, even if it had shut down as long as five years ago. And there's another thing. He thought the receipt didn't look right."

"In what sense?" Claire asked.

"The letterhead just didn't look professional enough. Bill said he's seen enough to know."

"Well," Jason mused. "Even if it is a phony receipt, that doesn't necessarily implicate Stefano. "His job was just to do the accounting and he could only work with what he was given. And you've already said there were indications that he tended to be on the careless side. He probably didn't even notice that there was anything funny about it."

Gerry looked deflated and like he was a little embarrassed that he hadn't thought of this himself. Claire had a resigned look on her face and Nell looked upset. *She's probably feeling sorry for Gerry that, after the risk he took and the considerable effort he expended, nothing much seems to have come of it,* thought Claire. *I better say something.*

Claire cleared her throat and began. "This is my eighth time trying to solve a murder mystery that the police have either given up on or insisted on going down one narrow track when other possibilities exist. What I have come to understand is why the police refer to a lot of the work they do as 'grunt work'. You have to go down one rabbit hole after another, and you spend more time 'eliminating people from your inquiries,' than you ever get to spend actually tracking down the perpetrator. And nine times out of ten it's not even your hard work that brings a killer to justice in the end. It's just by some stupid fluke that you never saw coming. So, Gerry, don't be disappointed. What you've done is very useful. Otherwise, we might've spent weeks speculating over Ian Turner instead of fully focusing on other possibilities. Oh, and by the way, have you called him yet? You did say that he made that angry phone call and we still don't know what he was so angry about."

"No, I haven't called him. I thought it was best to wait for this meeting so I could get some guidance on the best way to approach him about all this Also, if I come right out and tell him that I've checked his file——and I certainly can't tell him that I had a friend examine his confidential information——he could phone my superiors and I'd be in a lot of trouble. Remember, this was not my file and I'd never have been allowed to see it if I'd gone through the regular channels."

"I see the problem here," Claire said soberly. "And it makes what you've already done all the more valuable. It was certainly not something any of the rest of us could have taken on." Claire stopped for a minute to think and then went on. "I think the first thing you should do is find a time and a way to get all of those files back in their proper places."

Gerry ran his hand across his brow and rolled his head from side to side. "I'm certainly not looking forward to that," he said.

"Well, however long it takes you, I think you better do that before you call him. In fact," Claire said, "I don't think you should call him at all. For your own protection here, I don't think there should be any evidence of your footprint on this matter. You let me know when you have all the files safely back and then I'll call him. All I'll be able to say is that I'm following up on an entry in the family directory because of the murders."

"But wouldn't that be better coming from me?" Jason asked. "Since I'm part of the family?"

Claire was torn as to how to respond. She was not all that impressed with his handling of the two calls he'd described and seriously wondered what else he might have missed, both with those calls and the others he'd deemed not worthy of following up on. Finally, she said, "You make a good point, Jason. Let me think about it for a while and figure out what the best approach would be."

Claire turned back to Gerry and said briskly "Meanwhile, Gerry, you get those files back. I'd feel absolutely terrible if you ended up compromised in any way because you were kind enough to do all that for the sake of finding Mona's and Stefano's killer."

Claire turned again to Jason. "By the way, I thought you were going to follow up on Mona's ex-boyfriend, Leonard Reicher?"

"I'll do it this week," Jason replied, looking enthusiastic. And Claire just hoped that he wouldn't make a hash of it.

Claire and Nell had nothing much to report, but said their plan for the coming week was to follow up with Rosetta. She'd actually been named executor of the estate even though it would've been more logical to leave that task to a younger person. However, Stefano and Mona could agree neither on Stefano's brother nor Mona's sister, so Rosetta was the default choice.

"I think," Claire said, "particularly in light of what Gerry has uncovered, that we need to have a clearer picture of the family finances. It appears that Stefano splurged somewhat on his own wardrobe but from what I've heard, there's no other evidence of the kind of spending that would point towards a secondary source of income. I'm beginning to wonder, in fact, if they'd been going deeper and deeper in debt."

Jason perked up his ears when Claire said this. "To my knowledge, Mona has never said anything about this to Jocelyn, and I know that Stefano wouldn't have shared on such a personal matter. I don't know his brother well enough to ask him, but maybe ..."

"Don't," Claire said somewhat imperiously. "Let's just wait to see what Rosetta can find out."

And with that, the meeting ended and they all agreed to meet again the following week——same time, same place.

# - 17 -
## Progress, But Slow

It was a warm spring morning and Claire was busily going about her day's work with the twins when she heard the postman's mail drop. A letter had arrived from the office of the school board superintendent, and Claire opened it with trembling fingers. But when she'd finished reading it she smiled broadly. The superintendent had, as per her request, made a strong case against including Jessie in a high school context any longer, stating that because of her medical issues, the school system could no longer meet her needs.

Mr. Reese mentioned Jessica's frequent school absences because of her severe seizure disorder and the need to have oxygen near her at all times when she was present and the problem of having it administered by unqualified personnel whenever it was needed. He stated that they had obliged Jessie and her family as well as they could, even allowing her assistant to administer the potent anti-convulsant medication that she had to take 4 times in every 24-hour day. He pointed out that were likely some liability implications to this, that Jessie's long-term assistant had resigned, and that her replacement was very nervous about assuming this responsibility. The superintendent concluded by stating that at this point Jessie would be better served by a home-based day program in the community that could be tweaked to meet her needs on particular days.

Claire phoned Dan at work to tell him the news. He had left this school-leaving decision up to Claire but could see the potential benefits and now expressed his satisfaction that it was finally settled, and settled in time for her to make replacement plans for the upcoming fall term. Then she phoned Tia, still bubbling over with this life-changing news and they arranged to have lunch together that very day to catch up on this and other issues. Tia's response had been that this was too momentous a moment for her to miss and she was going to make arrangements with her supervisor to work until one and then take the rest of the day off. She would meet Claire at a restaurant near the school to maximize their time together and suggested that she phone Bethany to see if she could pinch hit with the twins for a couple of hours.

All was settled and by ten after one in the afternoon, Claire and Tia were seated together in a cozy booth of a Denny's restaurant just a block away from the hospital. "I can't believe it. I just can't believe it," Claire gushed. "No more rushing around frantically in the morning, my heart in my mouth, making sure Jessie's bag is packed with all she needs for the day and she being ready to go when the handi-bus arrives. No more boot camp. No more Dan coming home late every night because he has to help out in the morning with Jessie."

"But what about staffing? Are you sure you're going to get your replacement funding in time? What about an activity schedule?"

"The funding will come. I've already made tentative arrangements. I didn't start this process yesterday. Anyway, even if there is a gap period of a week or two I'd rather face that than the stress of the start of a new school year when there are so many issues to work out and I'm always living in fear that something will go wrong when Jessie's at school and new staff won't be able to cope."

"Boy. It'll be a whole new life for Jessie. You can bring her to visit Roscoe whenever you like. And to see my mom." Tia looked sad when she said this. Since the stroke, her mother had been much less communicative and just didn't seem to be there the way she used to be.

"I'd like that," Claire said softly. Marisa's present state upset Claire, too. Before the stroke she'd been such a dynamic and talented lady.

"What else do you have planned for Jessie's day program, Claire?"

"Oh, there are lots of options. There's the museum and the art gallery and…"

"Why would you take her to the art gallery when she can't see?"

"Good question. But one could use the same argument to eliminate movies, plays, even the zoo. In fact, you could take it even further," Claire added bitterly. "You could argue that there really is no point in taking Jessie anywhere. After all, it's not as if she can process incoming information efficiently, and even if she does make some sense out of some of it, most of it goes over her head. So why bother? Why have we even bothered all these years? Why did we lug her to Mexico and the mountains? What did she really get out of those trips for all the effort it cost us? In fact, if you wanted to take this argument to its logical conclusion you could ask what's the point of even keeping her alive?"

Tia wisely remained quiet. She recognized that Claire was on her soapbox again and any comment would only prolong the rant. She also knew that the person Claire was really arguing with was herself. These questions had come up anew for her after the birth of the twins when, after watching their rapid development, she had only fully realized for the first time just how much Jessie was missing.

After a suitable pause, Tia changed the subject. "How's the investigation coming? Do you need my help?"

"I've never had so many suspects to deal with and run into so many dead ends. I'm reduced to chasing down the Hail Mary candidates. Right now, I'm hoping to get in touch with Mona's former boyfriend——for no good reason except that he exists and may be accessible. Oh... there's also a former client of the murdered man who may or may not have cheated on his taxes."

"Doesn't sound too promising," Tia said, and decided it was time to change the subject again. They spent the next hour happily chatting along more personal lines about husbands, children and life in general. By the end of their visit, Claire felt refreshed and more energized to carry on with this increasingly tedious investigation than she'd felt before.

When Claire returned home, it was time to get back to the grind again and it was 8:30 in the evening before all was sufficiently calm in the Marchyshyn household for her to be able to pick up the phone and follow up on her next lead. She punched in the number and several rings later a brusque male voice came on the line.

"Yes. Who's this?"

"Hello. Am I speaking to Ian Turner?"

"Yes. Who are you?"

"My name is Claire Burke and I'm a friend of the de Felice/Amato family."

"Who?"

"I'm sure you've heard that Stefano and Mona Amato were recently murdered?" There was no response, so Claire soldiered on. A group of us close to the situation are supporting the family in finding the murderer and we found your number in their family phonebook. I'm just following up on all the entries there to see if anyone knows something that could help us."

"I don't even know them. My contact with Stefano Amato was strictly professional. He was my accountant."

"Well, I just wondered because none of his other clients are listed in his personal directory. We've been through the entire list now. You were the last one."

"Well, that's how it was. I've got nothing to tell you and I don't even know why you're calling. It said in the paper that it was a murder-suicide."

"Did you ever meet Mona Amato?"

"Uh, no-o-o. Why would I?——Look, lady, I don't know why you're calling me. I've already told you I don't know anything. Now, if you don't mind, I'd like to get on with my day." And with that he hung up the phone.

Claire sat with the phone in her hands feeling frustrated. But just then she heard Isaac's distinctive cry from the bedroom, and she had to put aside her mystery-solving activities for the time being.

# - **18** -

## Two "Detectives" Clean House

The next morning, Nell called for an update, knowing that Claire had been planning to call Ian Turner. Claire glumly reported her non-success and commented, "I really don't know where to go from here. If I had just one concrete thing to go on, I'd call Don McCoy, but I don't. He wasn't assigned to this case, but he might have some suggestions. It was seen as so cut and dried that a relatively new homicide investigator I've never heard of was assigned to it."

"Why don't you phone him anyway? He might suggest something."

"I don't know. All we really have is that discrepancy in Ian's file and that angry phone call. And neither of those things are things we're supposed to know about. I really don't want to cause trouble for Gerry."

"Well," Nell said thoughtfully. "From what you've told me, this McCoy guy is pretty smart and determined. And because it's not his case, and therefore not his conclusion that's being called into question, he might be more willing to help you than usual."

"And then there's the fact that he has kind of a soft spot for me," Claire could not help adding.

"Oh, I didn't know about that," Nell responded. She waited for Claire to add some details, but Claire said nothing more.

After a full minute passed with neither of them speaking, Claire said, "I'll think about calling, but do you have any ideas for anything else we can do to move this investigation along?"

"I think we should ask for access to the house and do a thorough search," Nell replied. "I know the police have already been through it, but they weren't there that long according to what Jason mentioned so I can't believe it was that thorough. They probably thought they had it all figured out as a murder-suicide."

"Okay, let's do that. Tomorrow is Bethany's day to take over with the twins so that would be the best time for me. What time would work for you?"

"Any time after ten. I don't like to rush in the mornings. One of the perks of being retired."

"I get it. I like time to get myself together in the mornings, too. Of course, I don't have that luxury right now. Anyway, I'll call Jason and ask if he'll drop off a house key to me and any directions I need for disarming the security system and I'll meet you there about eleven. Would that work?"

"Perfect," Nell replied. "I'll see you then."

"That's set then. I'll call you if there's any problem getting the key."

The next morning, Claire arrived at the Amato house at ten to eleven. She let herself in and carefully disarmed the alarm system. She looked around, deciding whether or not to take her shoes off. But the carpet looked well used and somewhat soiled, so she cleaned them carefully but left them on.

Claire walked into the kitchen and did a cursory glance around while keeping an eye through the window to check for Nell's arrival. Two minutes later, she was there, and Claire let her in. Nell stooped to remove her shoes, but Claire stopped her. "Just clean them well. You can see by the look of the carpets that they're going to have to be steam cleaned before they'll be able to rent or sell this house anyway. And remember what I told you about snooping. I know we have permission to be here this time, but it's always best to be prepared to run——just in case."

Nell looked at her and a shadow of anxiety flitted briefly across her round, usually cheerful-looking face. But then she grinned. "I think I'm going to like this snooping around business. It definitely breaks the monotony." You should have seen poor Gerry after his little adventure. He was jumpy and nervous for the whole week. That's why I said he's just not the type to take chances and skate close to the edge of the law or beyond it. He's just too upright and conscientious."

"I gathered that. That's why I'm surprised he's agreed with you getting involved, Nell."

"He was beginning to worry about me after I stopped working. So, like I said, he was happy I'd found a diversion. Also, I may be more relaxed than him, but he trusts me to be sensible in tricky situations and not to take too many risks."

"Hmm. I wish my husband was the same," Claire replied. "He worries obsessively whenever I do anything the least bit risky. And he certainly doesn't trust me to know how to keep myself out of trouble."

"Well, I don't know if it would work for you, but Gerry and I talk about everything. True, he didn't tell me in advance what he was planning to do that evening. But he told me the whole story the very next morning. How open have you been with your husband——Dan, is it?"

"Not very. He's been so intent on stopping me. That was why I was so surprised and impressed when Jason said he was going to talk directly and openly to Jocelyn about our proposed investigation and how we intended to proceed. First, I thought he was being very brave and ethical, and I should be the same with Dan. But then I remembered that he's a man with lots of testosterone and millennia of male patriarchy backing him up.

Men can always pull the 'your responsibility to the children' card to win any independence argument, but women can't do the same for some reason, even though men are often the primary breadwinners and without their support their children would certainly not do so well."

Nell just looked at her and said, "What about Jocelyn? Jason may be able to stand up to her on this matter but if he started telling her how much she could work and where she could go and who she could associate with and what she could do I don't think he'd come off so well."

"Maybe," Claire said sulkily, gritting her teeth.

Nell went on. "Jocelyn is assertive. I've seen her in action. She's confident, sure of herself——so she doesn't back down. I don't think a lack of testosterone or a history of male patriarchy has got in her way much."

Claire said nothing more and, after a short and rather awkward time passed, she suggested they get on with searching the house. Nell described herself as 'a kitchen person' and asked if she might start there. Claire agreed and stated that she'd start with the bedrooms and den and Nell might move on to the living room and foyer if she finished in the kitchen before Claire was through with her part. They'd already taken a quick tour through the house. It was an older home, perhaps from the sixties, with two bedrooms, a den, and a small family room in addition to the medium-sized kitchen and a combination living room-dining room.

During her earlier adventures, Claire had had various occasions to do home and office searches and she had a game plan in place. First, she stood in the doorway of the master bedroom and carefully scanned around it. Then she stepped into the modest ensuite bathroom. The entire room including the bathroom was carpeted with a dark, plush rug material, soiled and worn in places and obviously part of the original décor. *Whoever thought it was a good idea to have carpeting in bathrooms?*

Claire wondered. For the first part of her search, Claire knelt down and directed the powerful flashlight she'd brought along underneath the bed. But apart from a few dust bunnies there was nothing there to be found.

The next thing Claire did was to shine her flashlight under the tallboy and nine-drawer dresser units and to run the yard stick she'd brought with her underneath them. All she found for her trouble was a lone drop earring with a bright red stone in it. She stood up, laid it carefully on the dresser top and massaged her stiff knees for a few moments. Time to check the drawers. Claire worked carefully and neatly, feeling her way through all the material she could not see. In the middle drawer of the middle bank of drawers she felt a lump in a pair of navy winter snow pants. She carefully retrieved a small book and on opening it found that it was Mona's diary. She quickly scanned through it and found that the entries were intermittent and spanned the past three years, the length of her engagement and marriage, presumably.

Claire felt a momentary qualm about reading something so private but knew that if the police had found it, they'd have had no such concerns. This was a murder investigation, after all. She put the diary in her purse and moved on. Her next task was to thoroughly check out the bed. She stripped the sheets and blankets off, shook them and then carefully folded them to be respectful, even though she knew they'd have to be washed. Then she lifted the mattress on one side and shone the flashlight under, carefully searching for any unevenness on the bottom of the mattress or the top of the box spring, or any evidence of broken threads or mending on either surface. Nothing. She circled the bed and went through the same process on the other side. Nothing again. Then she lay flat on her back on the floor and peered under the box spring as best she could with the aid of the flashlight. After repeating this process on the other side and coming up empty, she neatly stacked the sheets and blankets back on the bed and began her search of the tallboy but again she found nothing.

After all that stretching and kneeling and wriggling around, Claire decided to do the bathroom next and tackle the closet last. It looked like a messy and complicated task. Most of what was there were the usual items found in such cabinets, but Claire did find a bottle of anti-depressant pills that had been prescribed for Mona the previous year. It was expired but there were still a few tablets left in the bottom and Claire couldn't help wondering why Mona hadn't taken them and had apparently not renewed the prescription.

The cabinets under the vanity unit held the usual cleaning materials and at first, she found nothing else of any particular interest. Her last task there was to sort through a box of odds and ends, and there she did find something of potential interest——it was the instruction booklet for a Girsan MC-28 semi-automatic 9mm pistol.

Claire sat back on her heels and thought for a minute. Then she re-searched the cabinets under the vanity with renewed focus and the aid of her trusty flashlight. There was no handgun there and no other place in the bathroom where it could be hiding. She attacked the bedroom closets with renewed vigor. Stefano's closet was relatively easy. It was neat and orderly and extra hooks and attachments had been installed to provide a place for everything. His clothing stock didn't appear to be extensive, but every item seemed to have style and to be in good condition. She checked shoe boxes and the storage boxes on his closet shelves but found no gun or anything else of interest.

Claire was about to begin her search of Mona's closet, the last of the bedroom tasks, but stopped when she heard Nell calling. She walked into the bedroom before Claire could respond and looked at her in surprise. Her eyes travelled up and down Claire and then around the room. "Wow!" she said, observing how dusty and disheveled Claire had become, the booklet sitting beside the earring on the dresser top and the stripped bed. "You've been busy. Get cleaned up and come for lunch. I found a few edibles in the freezer and it'll be ready in about two minutes."

Claire checked her watch and looked surprised. Then she headed for the bathroom to wash up. She noted that her breasts were starting to leak because she'd missed the twin's lunch feeding time and stuffed some Kleenex in her bra. Over lunch— a couple of TV dinners, some canned peaches, stale shortbread and bottles of flavored sparkling water—she told Nell what she'd found. Nell's eyes bugged out when she heard about the diary. "Can we read it?" she said, obviously not sharing Claire's compunctions about privacy.

"Not now," Claire responded. "No time. I'm going to take it home and go through it and if there is anything relevant to our investigation, I'll share it with you. After that, I think we should turn it over to her mother. We can't just leave it here for anybody to read, possibly——and perhaps most of all——her sister. I am sure Mona would hate that."

"Okay," Nell said softly, obviously thinking of the poor woman——her lost life and her lost dreams. They sat down to their meal and ate in silence for a few minutes. As usual, Claire, being the obsessive type once she got involved in something, hadn't realized how hungry she was. Finally, she turned to Nell and asked her, "Did you come up with anything?"

"Going through the pantry was quite a job," Nell replied. "Mona was certainly not the most organized person in the world. But just about everything that was there was what was supposed to be there—except..."

"What do you mean, 'except'?" Claire asked, a note of excitement in her voice.

Nell stood up and retrieved an empty box from the kitchen counter. She handed it to Claire. Claire scanned it and said excitedly, "Didn't you notice it's a box for a pistol?" She went back to the bedroom, grabbed the booklet she'd discovered, returned to the kitchen and compared the two. "They're for the same pistol," she declared. "See." Claire held the two items in front of Nell. "They both refer to a Girsan MC28 9-millimeter pistol."

Nell looked shocked but went back to eating her lunch.

"I don't suppose you found anything else in the kitchen cabinets or the freezer?" Claire asked.

Nell looked surprised. "Was I supposed to check the freezer? There's just food in there, I'm pretty sure——a lot of it."

Claire felt a moment of irritation. Tia would've checked, she knew. Aloud she said, "I'll check it out after lunch. I'm all grubby now anyway so I don't mind. Speaking of which, we'd better get started. I guess the first thing to do is clean up the lunch mess."

"I'll do that," Nell responded. "You can get started on the freezer." After a moment she added, "I did do the kitchen cupboards thoroughly. I even found some new food handling gloves and ran my hands through the sugar and flour and the dried beans. And I felt the brown sugar package all over to make sure there wasn't anything in there that wasn't supposed to be there."

"Good," Claire replied, and smiled brightly. She was feeling a bit bad. Obviously, Nell had picked up on her irritation over the freezer. Claire needed to be grateful for her help and to recognize that there was a learning curve to sleuthing. She hadn't started out as good as she was now and neither had Tia.

Moving all the stuff out of the freezer was a tedious and back tiring job. Claire checked the packages and finally had to conclude that there was nothing there, after all that work. Nell came in to check on her and she reported her non-findings. "I'll just chuck it all back in now," Claire said, "and then I'll move on to Mona's closet. I want to at least be finished with the master bedroom before we leave today. "Leave this to me," Nell said authoritatively. "I'll put it back in some sort of order so it'll be easier for whoever comes here to clean it out."

"Uh, that would be really nice, I guess," Claire replied.

"Thanks". She was relieved to be freed of the task but also thought that that wasn't generally the job of searchers who needed to use their time economically.

Claire opened Mona's closet door and two boxes immediately fell out on the floor. The closet was crammed and there didn't appear to be any discernible order there. After getting down on the floor and fumbling with the contents of the boxes for a few minutes, she called Nell who was just finishing with the freezer.

"I'll be there in a minute, Claire. Just wait." Two minutes later, Nell came in, took one glance at the situation, and advised Claire to sit down and wait for her to do some preliminary prep work. Although well aware of the time, Claire was happy to do so because the task truly was overwhelming.

Nell returned shortly, armed with a few cleaning supplies. Claire raised her eyebrows judgmentally, but Nell anticipated her response. "Just be patient," she said. "This is going to save time and it's also going to score us brownie points with Jocelyn who'll ultimately be the one who has to deal with this mess." Nell quickly and efficiently dusted the dresser and tallboy surfaces, the headboard and even the light fixture with the aid of the extender on the Swiffer duster. Then she dusted the floor including under the bed with the floor Swiffer. The whole effort took less than five minutes. Next, she moved the stack of sheets and one blanket to the dresser top and spread the other blanket out over the bed. "Now we have several surfaces on which to place items without just spreading the dust around and again, I think it will be appreciated. You never know when we might need to collect those brownie points down the road," Nell said cheerfully.

Claire was beginning to feel somewhat warmer towards Nell's efforts, recognizing that she had some of the same organizational efficiency as Tia and remembering how useful that had been in past searches. "You take the boxes down from the shelf, Claire, since you're taller than me and then we'll each take one box at a time and go through it and put it back before proceeding further.

Is that okay with you?"

"Sounds like a plan," Claire said happily, seeing light at the end of the tunnel. Claire and Nell worked their way slowly and systematically through the boxes. They found the usual collection of things people tend to save:    odd bits of school and other memorabilia from their childhood years, discarded articles that were at one point in their lives essential items like an old 'Walkman' portable CD player, souvenirs from various trips that Stefano and Mona had taken either together or alone, and other items that probably should've been discarded long ago but presumably held some sentimental value for one or both of them.

After another hour and a half had passed, the last box had been replaced and they sat down, side by side on the bed exhausted. The only box they'd kept out was the one containing six old photo albums and they were slowly flicking through them together.

"These ones of Mona at school seem to show that she was never really happy. She doesn't look like she felt a part of it. I wonder if she had any real friends growing up?" Nell commented.

"She wasn't very attractive; that's for sure," Claire observed. "She was on the hefty side even then but, of course, not as big as when I met her. You knew her longer, Nell. Had she put on much weight in recent years?"

"I would say so," Nell replied thoughtfully. "Maybe fifty pounds or so from the time I first met her three or four years ago. It was slow at first but then there was a big jump when she got pregnant and even more after Tammy was born."

"I wish we could talk to Jocelyn about what she remembers about Mona during her school years. Oh, well, we should be able to get some idea from Rosetta," Claire replied.

Finally, they picked up the last of the six albums and were surprised to find that it was a collection of pictures of Stefano and his family. "Why do you suppose his album is in Mona's closet?"

Nell asked.

"Well, certainly some of the stuff in those other boxes belonged to him as well," Claire pointed out. "I can't imagine that Mona wore boy's runners, for example——and that old t-shirt we found definitely belonged to a guy."

Nell and Claire looked at each other and simultaneously they glanced towards Stefano's closet. The door had been left open ("to air it out," Nell had recommended) and now they stared at the neat and rather dapper array of clothing and the shiny and carefully aligned row of shoes. "He clearly wanted that space all to himself," Claire concluded. "Mona could store all the leftover junk in her closet because her needs weren't as important as his. That must have been how he saw it."

Nell said nothing in reply, and they resumed their perusal of Stefano's photo album. "His baby pictures are cute. He had this kind of whimsical look," Nell commented.

Claire said nothing. She was eying the pictures of Stefano in his pre-adolescent childhood years. "He looks kind of weak and wimpy in these pictures," she mused, and then glanced at the wedding picture of Stefano and Mona on the dresser top. "But he really grew out of it. He's quite handsome in his wedding picture. I can really see why Mona went for him."

"You're right, Claire," Nell agreed. "Strange how kids can change when they grow up. One of my sons was an absolute peewee when he was twelve. Then he grew six inches in the next two years."

They went back to searching through the pictures but nothing else of any interest turned up and, in any case, it was definitely time to call it a day. "I think I'll take Stefano's album with me," Claire decided. "I feel like there's something here that I'm not seeing."

# - 19 -

## An Interesting Revelation

Claire awoke at 6:30 the next morning to the sound of Isaac, up for the day and wailing for his breakfast. She whisked him out of his crib and hurried from the room with him, closing the door behind her. Soon after their birth, Claire had observed how much easier life was if only one of the twins was demanding attention at a time and she'd done everything in her power to facilitate this. That had included setting up a baby changing station in the hall, which did little for the aesthetics of the home but much for her peace of mind. Her architect husband had objected vigorously at first but after enough disturbed nights and ridiculously early mornings he'd come around to her way of thinking.

Claire quickly changed Isaac and warmed his bottle. Soon he was settled peacefully in her arms sucking away. She thought again guiltily about the importance of nursing for strengthening his immune system. But she knew that he'd never be able to accept the breast when he was hungry and upset.

No doctor had been able to explain to Claire why breast feeding appeared to be such a chore for Isaac when his sister found it so easy and satisfying. It wasn't because of a tongue tie;

Claire had been quick to check that out after Tia's experience with her own baby, Marian. One doctor had mused about weak jaw muscles but that was all that had been offered as an explanation and no follow up had been suggested.

Claire was left with the nagging fear that if Isaac had this problem, then perhaps he had others as well, as yet undiagnosed. But at this stage of his development, all she could do was cope with the situation as best she could and hope that the few mouthfuls of breast milk he managed to ingest once he calmed down during a feeding would be enough to provide some immunity. And that no other developmental issues would emerge down the road.

Isaac had finished his bottle and was obviously still hungry. He had calmed down sufficiently to try the breast and nursed contentedly. Claire was able to shift her thoughts away from her fears and, since there was still no sound from Isabel, she was free to mull over yesterday's adventure.

Claire reviewed the findings of the day before: evidence of a recent gun purchase and a couple of photo albums. She'd come home yesterday afternoon feeling good about the day but now she realized that they hadn't really accomplished anything of significance. The box and instruction manual probably went with the gun the police already had in their possession and only pointed to the conclusion they'd already drawn, i.e., that Mona had shot her husband and then killed herself in a fit of depression, remorse or desperation. And the pictures? They didn't prove anything either. The observation that Mona looked unhappy and Stefano looked weak when they were children didn't lead to any firm conclusion about how and who they were when they died.

Isabel was awake now and Isaac had drifted off to sleep, a secret little smile on his milky mouth that touched Claire's heart. She placed him gently back in his crib and scooped up Isabel. Unlike her brother, Isabel grinned happily at her mother and waited patiently to be changed and nursed. After she was changed, the two of them sat contentedly in the family room,

Claire allowing her tired mind to drift into a neutral space as Isabel nursed. Dimly she was aware of Jessie's morning cry and the creaking of the bed as Dan arose to look after her. He'd taken over the responsibility of getting her ready for school after the twins arrived when it became clear that Claire couldn't manage the twins' morning routine and still get Jessie ready for school on-time.

*Where can I go from here to find the murderer? Maybe I've reached a dead end? Maybe I have a "mother-brain" and have lost my touch.* But just then the phone rang, pulling Claire away from her musing. She glanced at the clock. It was only 7:30. *Who can be calling this early?* she wondered. Fortunately, the phone was on the table beside her chair and Claire picked it up quickly before it could wake up Isaac or further disturb Isabel who was already acting restless and annoyed by this disruption of her time with her mother. It was a local area number, but one Claire didn't recognize. "Hello?" she said tentatively.

"Hello, is this Claire Burke?"

"Yes. Who's speaking, please?"

"Uh, this is Marco Amato ... Stefano's brother."

"Y-e-s," Claire replied slowly, her mind racing to catch up with this unexpected call. "We met a week ago. Have you thought of something that...?" she asked.

"Yes," Marco answered, more crisply now. "As it happens, I'll be free this afternoon. I was wondering if we could meet up somewhere?"

"Who's on the phone, Claire?" Dan called from the other room.

Claire quickly muffled the phone with her other hand, causing Isabel to cry out in annoyance. "I'll explain in a minute," she called back to Dan.

Turning her attention back to Marco Amato, she took her hand off the phone speaker and asked, "Would it be possible for you to come here? About two this afternoon?" and she quickly provided her address.

There was a long pause as the man thought this through, and Claire could here Dan trundling Jessie in her wheelchair towards the kitchen. Finally, speaking slowly as if still not quite sure, "I think I can manage that," and then, again very slowly, he repeated the address to make sure he had it right.

"Yes," Claire replied, rather abruptly. "I'll see you at two then."

"Alright, I'll ..."

"Bye for now," Claire replied brightly and hung up the phone just as Dan stuck his head in the door. He raised an eyebrow interrogatively.

"I'll explain once Jessie leaves and Isabel goes down for her nap," Claire said, and the two of them proceeded with their separate domestic tasks.

Half an hour later, Isabel asleep and Jessie on her way to school on DATS (the handicap transportation bus), Claire and Dan sat down in the family room with their coffee. She cleared her throat nervously and began. "Look, Dan, I've not been entirely honest with you ... about Mona's murder and what I've been doing to ..."

"I know," he interrupted. "I suspected as much and called Tia. She filled me in." Dan shook his head from side to side, half grinning and half grimacing.

"It's really important...and I haven't taken any chances," Claire blurted, looking at Dan fearfully but at the same time feeling anger toward the traitorous Tia.

Dan correctly read the look on Claire's face. By this point in their relationship, he'd become quite adept at deciphering her complex emotions. "Don't be angry at Tia, Claire. She has your best interests at heart and so do I. And it isn't just about the children. Also, she did tell me you were being cautious."

"I have to do this, Dan," Claire said emphatically. "The police are satisfied that Mona killed her husband and then herself and I know from what I've discovered to date that that just can't be true." Claire paused to allow Dan to respond but he said nothing. She went on. "That call this morning——that was from Stefano's brother. I tried to talk to him a few weeks ago about the situation but he either wouldn't or couldn't tell me anything at that point. I could see he was pretty upset. But today ... anyway, I've arranged for him to come here at two o'clock to share what he's willing to share now."

"I'll be here," Dan said grimly.

"Really?" Claire said, a note of relief in her voice. But then a second thought came to her. "I don't know if he'll talk in front of you."

"Don't worry. I'll just be in my study. And if the twins wake early from their nap, I'll take care of them."

"Thank you, Dan," Claire said gratefully. "And thank you for understanding." But then she had another thought. "But you had scheduled a meeting for today. You told me so. What about that?"

"I heard you on the phone, and I've already called and re-scheduled it," he replied neutrally.

Claire wondered what he was really thinking but decided to leave well enough alone. Inside she was feeling amazingly lucky that the fates had somehow aligned to bring her together with this loving and patient man. She was about to tell him so but then both twins woke up at once. Dan left her alone to deal with them and retreated to his study, apparently feeling that he'd been generous enough for one day.

# - 20 -
## Another New Direction

At two minutes after two, the doorbell rang. When Claire opened the door, she was struck by the expression on Marco' face. It was very different from how he'd looked at their previous meeting. She felt a chill——not fear——more like the thrill of the hunt. And an automatic set of behaviors honed from some of her previous "detecting" experiences took over.

Claire motioned Marco to a chair in her small living room and sat down opposite him. She looked at him expectantly but said nothing. This was not the time for the usual hostess behaviors. She could see that he was struggling and didn't want to say or do anything that would pull him back behind what she was sure was his normal façade.

A minute passed and then he hunched his shoulders protectively and began speaking. "I thought I should tell you a little about my brother. I don't know what you've heard about him, but I expect it wasn't all positive."

"I would appreciate that," Claire said, nodding her head encouragingly. Marco sat back in his chair and seemed to relax a little. After another minute passed, he began talking. "Stef didn't have it easy growing up. Neither did I for that matter but Stef had other problems I didn't have." He stopped talking then and Claire waited patiently for him to continue but she said nothing.

"Our parents...they're both gone now...died in their early sixties...heart attacks, both of them. High paying, high pressure careers so it makes sense. I don't think they had the time or energy to really care about us or even notice us much. They were both wrapped up in their work and their own interests——other high-powered friends, social obligations, cultural stuff ... I don't know. Sometimes I wondered why they even had us. I guess it was the thing to do in those days".

"I'm sorry," Claire said softly.

"Oh, I don't mean we were neglected or wanted for anything, except maybe their attention. There was always plenty of paid help and a nannie/tutor hired just for us. Whenever she told them there was something we needed, it was quickly provided. In fact, after a while she was given *carte blanche*. A special account was set up and then she just bought whatever we asked for——clothes, iPads, video games, pretty much whatever we wanted at the time. I played football in high school and I remember that Mandy—— she was with us for many years——came faithfully to all my games and reported back to the parents on how I'd done."

"Sounds pretty cold," Claire commented. "Did your parents ever talk to you directly about your games or school or your friends or anything?"

"Oh, yes. A couple of times a week they'd seem to notice us, and we'd have brief chats. Just the usual...'How's school? I hear you made a touchdown. What are your future plans?'...stuff like that."

"What about Stefano?"

"That's what I came to talk to you about, but I had to give you some background first," he replied, a defensive note in his voice.

Claire nodded quickly. "Of course... and thank you for that... thank you for sharing."

"Stefano did get their attention in the end——but not for any reasons he would've wanted. He would've preferred to be like me, to have been able to manage on his own and not have any big issues to face."

"What kind of issues?"

Marco hesitated before replying. "Finally, he said, "I'm only telling you this because I'm pretty sure you'll have heard some strong opinions about Stefano's short-comings and I wanted to present the other side of the picture," he said, almost angrily.

"And I want to hear it," Claire responded. "I don't feel at this point that I know enough about your brother to form any opinion of him one way or another."

"Good," he said, looking relieved. "Well, this is what I can tell you——and I'm sure he'd want you to know if it will help at all to solve his murder. Stefano was never strong like me. He was a fussy eater and always on the weak, spindly side when we were growing up. He wasn't assertive and was not very self-motivated. He just seemed to drift along. Stefano was bullied by the other boys because of the way he was but even more so because of how he looked."

"What do you mean 'how he looked'? I was in his house and saw his wedding picture on the bedroom dresser. He looked fine to me, kind of handsome actually." Claire blushed a little when she said this, not wanting to give Marco any wrong ideas.

"Oh, that's what he looks like now——or did before he died." Claire saw Marco's shoulders drop when he made this self-correction. "But that's not what he looked like as a child." Marco pulled a picture out of a folder he'd brought with him and held it out for Claire to see. "This is him when he was about eight."

Claire peered at the picture. It was small and dark and a bit wrinkled. But she could see that Stefano had hardly been an appealing child. His ears stuck way out and he was weak chinned. It was hard to relate it to the wedding picture of the adult he'd become.

"What happened?" was all she could think to say, feeling at a loss for words.

"Do you mean 'what happened' to cause him to look like that or 'what happened' that he didn't look the same as an adult?"

"Both, I guess ... no—just the adult change," Claire stuttered. "He wasn't deformed as a child. Just ... er, just a little on the different side."

"He was different enough that his classmates teased him unmercifully. He might've been bullied anyway because he was always on the timid side——but those ears and that chin really gave them a lot of ammunition."

Claire peered closely at the picture Marco had brought. "The ears do stick out quite a lot, but I've seen other kids who looked like that and they survived. And the chin really doesn't look that severely retracted."

"Not then so much, but it got a lot worse in his early teen years," Marco retorted. "And there were other things as well that set him apart. He was always on the thin, frail side and short for his age. An additional problem was his food allergies, so he was often home with a stomach-ache or because he'd developed an ugly rash. And then he was timid and could never fight back when the school bullies picked on him. All in all, he was seen by his classmates as a real dweeb."

"Were you in the same school as him?"

"Yes, part of the time. I am——or was——three years older than him so he was still in the elementary grades when I moved on to junior high which was in a separate wing of the school. Also, I went to a different school altogether for high school and by the time he got there I was leaving for university. So, I really wasn't much help to him," Marco explained, his voice husky.

"It was even worse than that," he went on. "Not only was my presence in his life of no help to him; it actually made things worse. To Stefano I appeared to be everything he was not. I was tall and strong, and I did well at school and was good in sports. Even though our parents were preoccupied with their own lives and had no more time for me than they had for him, I could feel their quiet pride in my successes, and I know that Stefano felt it too. That just made him feel like even more of a loser."

"But what happened then? He didn't look the same as an adult that he did as a child so your parents must have noticed something and done something."

"Yes, well——*they* didn't notice. Mandy noticed. Stefano used to talk to her. He had to talk to somebody who would really listen. He told her about what the kids said about his ears, probably when he was seven or eight. She must have done some research, because she talked to our parents about the issue and explained how there was an operation to pin ears back and showed them some before and after pictures that she'd found on-line."

"So how did they respond to that?"

"They told her to go ahead and find a good specialist and then to take him to the family doctor and get a referral."

"Isn't that something they would expect the parents to do?" Claire asked.

"You'd think," Marco replied angrily. After a pause he went on. "Anyway, Mandy managed to arrange it all. She had been with us several years by then, and as I recall my parents actually went to a lawyer and got her signed on as a co-guardian so she could take care of these kinds of arrangements. She found a specialist and took Stefano in for the appointments and in May of his grade three year he had the operation. He didn't go back to school for the rest of that year and by the fall when he returned, his ears looked perfectly normal and nobody teased him about them anymore."

"That must have been a great relief to him. Was he okay after that?"

"He seemed better. But he still didn't have any friends and he was still on the quiet, timid side. However, he got through the rest of elementary school okay. It was only when he got to junior high that things started to get difficult for him again."

"Why was that?"

"Kids are 12, 13, 14 or 15 at that point, and they're starting to grow and change. Stefano didn't grow much during those years, but his face was changing, and his receding chin became more and more obvious. He had never really fully recovered his confidence from his earlier experience of being teased so much and he seemed to just draw more and more into his shell.

"Mandy was still with us at that time, and she was the one who took us for our regular dental checkups. That year, the dentist noticed that Stefano's teeth weren't meshing properly, and they were starting to get ground down as a result. He referred him to a dental surgeon for consultation and Mandy went ahead and made the appointment."

"And your parents just went along with this?"

"Oh, they would've been fine with that, but the dentist's receptionist informed Mandy that at least one of the parents would have to be present at the consultation interview and, as usual they objected, saying they didn't have time and the date was inconvenient. But Mandy was ready for them. She'd been doing some research of her own and showed them before and after pictures of teenagers with a retracted chin who'd had the jaw reconstruction.

"It was Stefano's father who decided this was something that Stefano needed to do because he saw immediately what a difference it would make to his appearance. The main reason for getting it done from the dentists' perspective, that it would improve his teeth meshing and protect them from wearing down his teeth, didn't even concern him. He dismissed all that as B.S. concocted by dentists so they could make big bucks. I remember him saying that at the supper table."

"So did your father go to the interview with Stefano?"

"Oh, no. He told my mother that she'd better go. He argued that that was the kind of job a mother was supposed to do."

"Wait a minute. How did Stefano feel about all this?"

"He didn't want to have the operation. He was scared. But my dad kept bullying him, telling him it was for his own good and not to be such a chicken shit."

"Lovely," Claire muttered.

"Anyway, Stefano had the jaw reconstruction in January of his grade ten year, and he didn't go back to school until sometime in March. Meanwhile, his hair was growing longer, and he refused to have it cut. By the time he returned to school the scars at the top of his jaws had faded quite a lot and his long hair hid them pretty well."

"Did he look very different?"

"Yes, but his face was still swollen. The dentist explained that it takes a long time to recover from such a major operation. Also, Stefano was growing and changing, and he had a few pimples, so his face was often red and puffy in places from that. One way or another, I don't think the other kids noticed the improvement that much then."

"But did he fit in better at school then?"

"No, if anything it got worse. And from the way he talked, I'd say that he didn't even try. He told me that he hated the place and everyone there."

"But he was in high school then, in a different school, right?"

"Yes, but it wasn't as if he could start over fresh. A lot of the kids from his old school were there, 'contaminating the place' as he told me."

"But boys aren't like girls, always gossiping and forming cliques. Didn't he get along with some of the new guys?"

"No, but I'm pretty sure that was more about him than about them. He usually had a scowl on his face and pushed people away."

"I guess the psychological damage was something you couldn't operate away," Claire said sadly.

"No. That about says it. Anyway, about a month after he returned to school, the school counsellor got involved and he called our parents in for an interview to discuss the situation with

Stefano."

"Did they go?"

"Oh, they pretty well had to at that point. Stefano was caught trying to set the school on fire. The school principal called them and told them they could either work with the counsellor to try to deal with the situation or the principal was going to refer the matter to the police and file charges and have the juvenile court deal with him."

"I guess that got their attention," Claire said grimly.

"That it did."

"What was Mandy's input into all this?"

"Oh, she left us shortly after his operation. We were really too old for a nanny at that point, but my parents would've kept her on, 'to support Stefano' as they put it. But really it was to run interference and support them. She had a boyfriend and was planning on getting married. But also, I think she was sick and tired of playing mother and father to a teenaged boy when she was only in her late twenties herself."

"That must have been really hard on Stefano."

"I agree——but he never talked about it. However, once he was back at school——and he hadn't wanted to go back but my parents insisted——he seemed to do everything he could to sabotage the situation. The fire setting was just the last straw. But apart from that, he was often late, insolent to the teachers and he refused to complete homework assignments. He seemed determined to fail."

"So how did the counsellor propose dealing with the situation?"

"He said it was beyond his skill set and recommended to my parents that they seek professional counselling for Stef outside the school, maybe even take him to a psychiatrist or psychologist for a thorough assessment of his emotional state."

"How did they respond to that?"

"They came from that meeting very upset, my father in

particular. He was outraged that anyone should think that his son had emotional problems. He railed at Stefano at the supper table, told him to get his act together, to stop being such a wimp. Dad told him that he was an embarrassment to him, and he better shape up or else."

"And what did that accomplish?" Claire asked dryly.

"Stefano just got that sulky look on his face again and stomped out of the room without finishing his supper. Mother ran after him, but he slammed the door in her face."

"Was that the end of it?"

"No. The next day the principal called my dad again and told him that if they didn't come back to see the counsellor within the next three days, he was still going to refer the whole matter to the police."

"Did they go back?"

"Yes, and the second time I guess it went a little better. The principal must have also had something to say to the counsellor. Carl was his name, I believe. Anyway, this Carl had apparently been doing some research and this time he suggested that my parents hire a lifestyle coach for Stefano. He explained that this coach could provide Stefano with assertiveness training and this would give him the skills to stand up to others when he was bullied, which was apparently still happening. My mother, Chiara, was surprised by this because Stefano never said anything about it at home. But, of course, he never had talked to mom and dad directly about his problems. He only ever talked to Mandy about the bullying. And by that time, like I said, Mandy was gone."

"Did the counsellor suggest anybody in particular?"

"No, and when I think about it now, I'm realizing that the counsellor really was on the weak, ineffective side. So-called 'lifestyle coaches' are not registered with any official body as far as I know. I've seen their ads in the papers and on television. They basically promise to help you achieve a better life but are sketchy about the details. Anyone can take a 6-month lifestyle coach training session on-line and get an official looking certificate, but I certainly wouldn't turn one of my children over to them."

"Well, did they do that?"

"He did——Giaco."

"Jacko?"

"That's my father's nickname. G-I-A-C-O. It's short for Giacomo."

"Okay," Claire replied. "But what did your mother have to say?"

"She wanted him to see a psychologist. She talked about 'getting to the root' of the problem."

"And how did Giaco respond to that?"

"He literally exploded, as I recall. Said the boy had been coddled too much. Should never have had that female nanny for so long. He said that Stefano had been feminized. He told her that he was going to find somebody who could make a man out of him."

"And was Stefano listening to all this?"

"He was in his room at that point. It was right after supper and he'd already left the table. But I'm sure he heard. I'm sure the neighbours even heard the way dad was shouting."

"So did your dad find somebody?"

"Yes, he did."

# - 21 -

## The "Interventionist"

"Dad saw this ad on TV and contacted the person who ran it, Don Marron. He then went to his office alone to interview the guy. He wouldn't let my mother come. Said it was time for him to take charge and straighten out this mess."

Claire shook her head and asked, "What arrangement did he come to with this Don?"

"Stefano was to stay in school and visit Don twice a week after school at his office."

"How long did that last?"

"Pretty much the rest of that school year and through the summer and the fall term, as I recall. And then he saw him a few times that next spring because of something else that happened."

"Did Stefano ever share what they talked about?"

"Only with me——and more at the beginning than towards the end. As the months passed, he grew more and more … self-contained, I guess one could say. He wasn't pouty or nasty, or not very often anyway. And there were no more reports of problems from the school. He just became kind of secretive and aloof."

"Can you remember anything specific he might have told you

about what this lifestyle coach was advising?"

"Yes. The first thing Stefano was told was that it was very important not to show your true feelings——that you have to 'fake it until you can make it."

"Did he have any suggestions for Stefano as to how he was supposed to do that?"

"Yes, I suppose you could call them suggestions. He told Stefano he should start by going around wearing a mysterious half-smile, like something was secretly amusing him. And he should be sure to stay very calm on the outside no matter how he was feeling on the inside."

"And what was he supposed to do after the smile?" Claire asked incredulously.

"If somebody asked him why he was smiling, he was just supposed to reply, 'Oh…no reason' and then, since the other person had broken the ice, he should ask them questions, get them talking about themselves.

"He told Stefano he should start by practicing on others—— family members, neighbours, even the nannies he passed in the street pushing babies in their strollers. Just get their attention with that mysterious half smile and then if they said anything to him or smiled back, he could make some bland comment like 'nice day' or 'looks like rain'. He should keep practicing until he got good at it and could do it smoothly. 'Practice makes perfect' was Don's mantra.

"Was that it? All he had to offer?"

"No. Another suggestion he had was for Stefano to download two or three season's worth of episodes of the old TV show, *Happy Days*. He was to pay particular attention to the Fonz character, to his body language. They watched a couple of episodes together and Don pointed out to him things like posture, eye contact, a certain air of self-assurance. He told him he had to be more subtle than that because the Fonz character was kind of a caricature and people would see right through him if he simply aped that act. But that the general principles applied."

"What about girls, girls at school? How was he supposed to get to know them that way?"

"Oh, Stefano was almost fifteen at that point and he was pretty preoccupied with girls——just like we all were at that age. But Don told him to wait. He had to perfect his technique before he approached a girl and expressed interest in her. Otherwise he'd just 'poison the waters', as he told him."

"'Poison the waters'? So what was he supposed to do in the meantime?"

"Keep practicing and also observe, observe, observe. He was supposed to watch how other guys approached girls and how they responded."

"And then?"

"The summer passed and oh … I forgot. Dad got him enrolled in a gym and working with a physical trainer over the summer. He also sent him to a tanning studio. Fortunately, Stefano never had the acne problems I had. I don't know why since he had all those allergies and everything but that's how it was. Anyway, by the time of his grade eleven year, he'd grown 3 ½ inches, and was average height——about 5'11" or so. His muscles had developed, and he'd put on a little weight and had quite a nice tan, so he didn't look too bad at all."

"How did the other kids respond when he went back to school?"

"I don't really know. Stefano didn't talk much to me about his life at that time. But he seemed a little happier and he'd occasionally hang out with a couple of the guys at school. Oh. There's something else I forgot to mention. Stefano had never been very interested in clothes and for years it had been Mandy who'd gone out and bought him what he needed whenever a new school year started. But that summer Dad actually took time off work and took him shopping. They were gone most of the day and when they finally got home Stefano had a whole new wardrobe with him. Apparently, Don had talked to Giaco about the kinds of clothes and accessories Stefano should have, what were the in-things for guys his age, and they'd worked methodically at acquiring them.

"What about girls?"

"Well, that he did talk about. I remember. He came home one day that fall all excited and came into my room to talk to me. I think it was because he felt that he had something to teach me for a change, instead of the other way around."

"What was that?"

"I gather girls had been the main topic of conversation for Stefano and Don that fall——how to approach them and how and when to make a move on them." Claire shuddered visibly when she heard this, and Marco noticed. "Do you want me to tell you?" he asked, "or should we just move on?"

Claire thought about this for a minute and then said "I think you better tell me. I need to understand his psychology and his *modus operandi* if I'm to get to the bottom of what happened."

"Well, he started by telling Stefano that he should always start by asking her about herself and not talking about himself. 'Girls like to talk about themselves,' he told Stefano. He should pick one girl to practice on."

"And how did he do that?"

"From what he let on, I gather that girls had mostly just ignored him. But one girl had intervened the previous fall when the class bully and his goons were pushing Stefano around. She had given him some Kleenex to wipe the blood off his face and then had walked him home because he seemed so shaky. She'd even put her arm around him. He told Don about her and Don thought she'd be a good one to start on and told him what to do."

"What was the goal?" Claire asked tonelessly.

"He was to get her to the point where she was willing to have an intimate relationship with him," Marco said primly. He was obviously a little embarrassed to be having this kind of conversation with a woman he hardly knew.

"He was to go from underdog to overlord. How did that work out?"

"Don explained that it would be a slow process and Stefano needed to be patient. He would have to get her 'ready' first."

Claire shuddered, reflecting back on some of her early dating experiences. *What was real, caring——and what were just calculated moves?* she asked herself. The world suddenly seemed to be a darker, meaner place.

"Do you want me to go on?" Marco asked quietly.

Claire nodded but said nothing. She suddenly felt very tired.

# - 22 -

## How to Woo, the Don Marron Way

"'First you get her talking,' Don had told Stefano, and then, when she's talking to you easily, you slowly begin to make some affectionate gestures.'

"'How do I do that?' my brother had asked him. 'Well, 'you should be moving around by then,' Don told him. Maybe walking with her between classes or even outside, opening doors for her. And then, as she goes through the door, you place your hand gently in the middle of her back, just ostensibly to guide her through the door. After a while, the gestures become a little bolder, maybe placing your hand on her hip, not too far forward or too far back. Nothing gross or suggestive. And if she's wearing a short blouse, kind of the style these days, you might place your arm around her waist and just let your thumb and first finger accidentally reach under the edge of the blouse and touch her skin lightly. Stuff like that," Marco said, his face reddening.

"And did he expect Stefano to remember all that?" Claire asked.

"No. They practiced."

"How?"

"Well, that was kind of the funny part. Don had purchased a store dummy——you know, the kind you see in the window all dressed up in the latest style. He called her 'Sally'. She was dressed in that type of short blouse I described and a short skirt. Well, I won't go into detail, but he showed Stefano all the subtle moves to get her 'ready', as he said, without being heavy-handed about it."

"Like a pedophile grooming a victim," Claire exclaimed in disgust.

Marco didn't respond to that but just went on with his story. "Stefano started slow, he said, but it didn't work. She was too attached to her father and didn't want to do anything that could hurt him, is what she told Stefano. He almost lost his confidence then, but Don talked him through it. 'Don't let on how you feel,' he was told. 'Never let them know. Always keep them guessing, off balance'. Well, long story short——he finally succeeded, and they had this little affair."

"Little?" Claire asked, disgusted by this trivializing of something so important. "Why little?"

"Because, as Don explained, the next thing that Stefano had to practice was breaking it off. It was important for him to learn how to do this, to always be in control of the situation, to maintain mastery over the women he went after. He must never let himself become vulnerable, get sucked in."

"Sucked in?" Claire asked weakly.

"Yes. Stefano had to learn when to leave and how to leave. They spent a whole session together on 'the break-up talk'. Dan had him practice it on the dummy but the real practice, he said, could only take place with the girl."

"The girl? What was her name?"

"Marta, I think. Something like that. Anyway, Stefano really liked her, and he didn't want to break it off with her. But Don insisted. He said that was the only way he was going to acquire mastery, to learn how to retain control over any future relationships he had. Unfortunately, the lesson in how not to go too far into a relationship before breaking it off came later, after the relationship was well established. Stefano had already talked about marriage with her down the road, built a picture of their future plans, their future life together. Then he broke it off. But he didn't have the skills. It was very sudden. He didn't give her time to get used to it."

"What happened to the girl?"

"He heard later that she went into a rebound relationship with some older guy, not in school. She got pregnant. Not by him. Don had trained him well about that, really drilled that into him. 'Don't get yourself into a bad position; don't get trapped' he'd said. Anyway, the girl hung herself in her bedroom. Apparently, her father found her. Her mother had died when she was young. She'd already felt vulnerable, abandoned——and that was probably why Stefano had been able to develop the relationship he had with her. Anyway, she apparently left a note and Stefano found out about it because the police contacted him as part of their follow-up. She said in the note that she didn't know how to tell her father about the baby. She couldn't bear to let him down like that and she saw no other way out."

"How did Stefano feel about that?"

"Well, first he felt bad, but Don coached him. 'It's nothing to do with you,' he told him. 'Not your fault'. There are these saps in the world, walking victims just waiting for it to happen. Not your problem. If it hadn't been you it would've been somebody else. Besides, you're not that guy. Never be that guy. Protect yourself."

"Okay," Claire said, feeling slightly sick. "Then what happened?"

"Oh, there were others, lots of others. He became quite the Lothario."

Claire didn't even want to hear about it. She got the picture and quickly changed the subject. "What about school?" she asked. "You said he was doing bad, falling behind."

"Yes, but Don talked him through that. Got him to stuff away those feelings, pretend he never had them. After Giaco bragged to his wife about the dummy and about how clever Don was, Chiara didn't want her son to see Don anymore. She thought it had been a mistake. But the father insisted. He actually thought that the dummy was a good idea and talked to Stefano about it, telling him what a man he was becoming. I know Stef felt close to him for the first time at that point.

"I guess Stef must have told Don how mother was feeling, because Don quickly changed directions after that. He started focusing on Stefano's academics but put his own spin on it, one that Stef could accept. He agreed with him that school was a big bore and that teachers were just a bunch of dumb losers who were there because they couldn't do anything else in the real world. But then he pointed out that school was a means to an end and the better he did, the more options he'd have. He helped Stef to think ahead to what he wanted. He put it to him like this. It was all 'crap', but he needed his share of the pie. How could he get an education that would get him that with the least effort? He talked about cost-benefit ratio. Stef always had a flare for math, so Don zeroed in on that and even did a little research.

"A couple of weeks later, Don came up with the idea of a career in accounting for him. He told Stefano that he could do it in steps, become a bookkeeper first and earn some money so he could keep his social life going. Plow on to get a degree and watch for opportunities. Don taught him how to use some of the same skills he'd acquired in seducing girls to seduce potential employers; listening closely to them, encouraging their confidences finding out their weak spots, then using them to his advantage to get ahead at work."

"Did it happen that way? Is that why he appeared to have done so well?"

"I think so, but after a while he quit talking to me about things. I suspect that was Don's doing, too, but I have no way of knowing. I confronted Stefano about it once, but he just blew me off."

"How did he end up with Mona? If he had all those courting skills, I'd have expected him to find somebody better," Claire blurted.

Marco raised his eyebrows.

"I mean," Claire went on, flustered, "somebody prettier, more polished, somebody with her own career."

"You would think," Marco agreed. "But, you see, Don was hardly a psychologist. It's not as if he actually helped Stef to heal from all he'd been through during his school years. He just taught him how to cover it up, to bury it so he'd be more acceptable to others and could get ahead in life. I think Stef actually cared about Mona. He saw a vulnerability in her and a brave front that he could relate to. He felt comfortable and safe with her. He thought he could be the man he was instead of the one he pretended to be with her. At least that's how I see it. But like I said, he never talked to me directly about her."

Claire saw him impatiently brush away a tear, so she thought it was time to change the subject. In fact, she decided it was time to end the interview. She was feeling overwhelmed and just wanted to be alone to think about all she'd learned. Also, she wanted to talk to Jessie about it.

# - 23 -
## Jessie and Tia Help

That evening, Claire mechanically put supper on the table and fed Isabel while Dan fed Isaac. Meanwhile Alice, a new evening helper, fed Jessie with some occasional advice from Dan. After supper, Claire turned to Dan. "Maybe the twins can go to bed tonight without a bath," she said. "I need to spend some time alone with Jessie."

Dan looked at her. He could tell something was wrong and by what he'd overheard of her interview with Marco Amato he was pretty sure he knew what. He nodded his head and said, "Don't worry about them. I'll get them to bed. Just nurse them while I put Jessie on the loveseat."

Claire nodded tiredly and then turned to Alice. "Please do the dishes and clean up the kitchen tonight. I'll be in the family room with Jessie when you're finished." Soon she was sitting beside Jessie on the loveseat, the gas fireplace was on and they had a blanket over their laps to keep them cozy. Dan had some soft music playing in the background and she found a glass of white wine sitting there for her on the table on her side of the loveseat. *Don Marron wouldn't understand the kind of relationship that*

*Dan and I have,* Claire thought to herself. *He probably wouldn't believe that it could even exist.*

Claire pulled Jessie onto her lap and wondered how much longer she'd be able to do that. Jessie was almost as tall as she was now and still growing——although she was considerably lighter. Jessie made her happy sound, but Claire said nothing. She just held her close and rubbed her face in Jessie's hair. As the minutes passed, she could feel a cleansing of her spirit as the ugliness of the afternoon talk moved gradually away into a more distant place where it could no longer overwhelm her.

Finally, Claire was able to talk. She didn't want to tell Jessie what she'd learned even though she realized full well that Jessie wouldn't be able to understand it except for picking up on the tone in Claire's words. Still, Claire felt it was too ugly to say out loud. Instead she said, "Some men do terrible things to women, Jessie. And you know what? If a man ever did that to you, I'd kill him."

Jessie squirmed in her arms, alarmed by the intensity of Claire's words. "Yes, I would," Claire declared again, and held Jessie even more tightly, stroking her arm in a fiercely protective manner.

Whatever Jessie might have been thinking, she was unable to say but she gurgled appreciatively. Claire loosened her hold, rocked Jessie back and forth in her arms and felt all the rage and hurt flow out of her and land in a cold puddle at her feet. She pulled the blanket up higher over both of them, like a protective wall. Then she picked up a young adult book Dan had chosen from Jessie's collection and started reading to her. *It's always this way,* she thought to herself. *Jessie heals me when nobody else can, not even Dan.*

They spent the next 30 minutes together, just cuddling and reading. Then Alice came to report that the kitchen was now clean and to take Jessie away for her bath and preparation for bed. Claire gave Jessie one last kiss and then walked away,

heading for her bedroom and feeling much lighter than she'd felt
since that terrible, ugly interview. But she still wasn't ready for
her usual evening conversation with Dan. Instead she called Tia.

"Hi, Claire," Tia responded, having noted the number on the
call display. "I was just thinking about you. You know tomorrow
is my day off. Any chance of a visit?"

"That's exactly why I'm calling," Claire said exultantly. It was
rare to hear Tia actually suggesting a visit since she was usually
so busy with her husband, children and work that she hardly
seemed to have any time left over for Claire.

"What's happening with the case?"

"Things," declared Claire ominously. "That's what I need to
go over with you."

"Good. What time can you come?"

They made their arrangements and the next morning found
Claire, with the twins in tow, on Tia's doorstep. "Come in," Tia
welcomed them cheerily. Marion's in the living room and she's
anxious to see the little playmates you brought her."

Soon they were all settled comfortably in Tia's living room
and, caught up in one of those magical moments in time that
occur rarely and unpredictably, while the three children played
happily together with the toys that Tia had set out for them. The
fact that Marion was a full two years older than the twins didn't
seem to matter to any of them.

Claire took the opportunity to update Tia on all that had been
happening with "the case." And thanks to Jessie's calming effect
she was able to summarize the peculiar story of Stefano's
emotional development. When she finished, Tia just looked at her
and said, "Well, that's very interesting but where are you going
to go from here?"

Having only just emerged from this latest rabbit hole, Claire
hadn't thought that far ahead but now she suddenly realized what
she must do. "If he treated women that badly, he's bound to have
made enemies along the way:  husbands, boyfriends, even
parents. What I need are some names. But Marco seemed to

suggest that Stefano stopped talking to him about such things before he even finished school, so I don't think he knows much about any relationships Stefano may have had in his adult life."

"What leads were you planning to follow before you got this unexpected visit from this Marco person?"

"Um, it's getting so complicated I almost forget. Oh, yes. There's this Ian Turner person I told you about. He had Stefano doing his income taxes and had submitted a $3000.00 bill for a new furnace from a company that does not appear to exist. And Stefano went ahead and submitted it and now Ian's getting audited by the CRA.

"That's always very upsetting, but would it be sufficient reason to commit a double murder?"

"No, I guess not. And whether he's guilty of fraud or not is definitely not my problem."

"Good. Let's move on then."

Claire sat back and felt herself relaxing more than she had in quite a while. She realized now how much she'd missed Tia's involvement in this case, the sharing of responsibility and decision making with her. She felt her head starting to clear as she relaxed and tried hard to recall the other loose ends that she knew were out there. "There's a Sheila Her…Herman, I think. She is a librarian that Mona used to see before she married and moved away. Apparently, Mona phoned her a couple of months ago suggesting they get together but then she never got back to her."

"And why would this be relevant to your investigation?" Tia asked in her usual crisp, incisive way.

"I don't know. Now that you put it that way it sounds like this was more like a business relationship, a relationship of convenience when she visited the library and wanted certain books. I don't know why Mona would call her out of the blue like that, though. That is what's bothering me."

"You did tell me that Mona was feeling alone and

overwhelmed and was coming across to her husband and mother as very needy and not able to cope on her own with her daughter. Do you think maybe she was just grasping at straws, reaching out to others she'd known in the past to try to renew acquaintances and possibly glean some measure of understanding and support from them."

"Y-e-s, that makes sense. I know she also reached out to Sadie, an old school chum——and I'm pretty sure that Sadie had nothing to do with the murder. Now that I really think about it, I suspect that it's just the same for this librarian person."

"Fine … but do you have any real leads to follow?"

"Okay. Mona had an old boyfriend and she broke up with him after she met Stefano. According to Sadie who knew him——she and her boyfriend used to double date with Mona and this Leonard person——he was very upset and unhappy about the break-up."

"That sounds more promising. How are you following up?"

"Well, actually I asked Jason to get in contact with him."

"Why did you do that? You told me he hadn't done a very good job on the other follow-ups he did."

"I don't know. There seemed to be too many directions for me to follow up on my own. And at that point Dan still didn't know I was involved, and I was trying to keep it that way."

Tia shook her head censoriously but said nothing and Claire went on. "I think I'll call Jason and if he hasn't made contact with Leonard yet, I'll tell him that I want to do it. The trouble is he might be offended. He wanted to help, and he's been very supportive. In fact, without his initial support I don't know how I could have even got this far."

Tia raised her eyebrows. "That's very nice——but is he supporting you because he likes your or feels sorry for you or something? Or is he supporting you because he wants to find out who killed his sister-in-law?"

Claire shook her head to rid herself of some of her befuddlement. "He wants to know who really killed Mona and

Stefano. He doesn't believe that Mona did it."

"Fine, then your involvement in the investigation serves his purpose. You don't owe him. He owes you. You need to call him ASAP and tell him you'll be following up with this Leonard. And if he feels miffed, that's his problem. You have an established history of finding murderers. He does not."

"Okay," Claire said weakly, once again grateful for Tia's clear head. And that reminds me. There was a listing in the family phone book for the Cyber family, Jason said and when he phoned, he talked to the man, Sid. He thought that the name, Sid Cyber, was pretty suspicious and the man was very impatient with him and didn't think that Jason had any business calling him."

"You said 'family'. Is that how he was listed in their phone book?"

"Actually, Jason said it was listed as 'Cyber Fam'——but there were no other listings like that."

"Does this Sid person have any children?"

"No. He told Jason that it was just him and his wife."

"Have you seen that phone book yourself?"

"No. Jason only gave us a copy of the entries."

"I suggest you ask him for the phone book so you can examine that entry yourself. It doesn't sound right. Maybe 'fam' referred to something else."

"You might be right. I'll definitely do that."

"Any other leads?"

"No, not at present. But I'd really like to know what other women Stefano was involved with. I'm feeling like that would be the most productive avenue to explore but nobody seems to know for sure if he even had any other affairs or if he's carried on with anyone else since he's been married."

"Can't help you there but if you find one, that might lead you to others. Why don't you start by talking to the Cyber wife? If that Sid was as hostile on the phone as Jason reports, maybe he was covering up something?"

"Okay, I'll do that."

"Is there anybody else who might know——Mona's mother or a friend maybe? I tell things to you that I probably wouldn't tell a brother or a sister if I had one."

"He doesn't seem to have had any close friends. I told you how we went through the family phone directory and came up empty."

"Yes, but he might not have entered the number in a directory. People are more and more in the habit of storing numbers on their phones. Did you check his phone?"

"No. At the time our little group was discussing this, Jason still didn't have the phone back from the police although I know he has it back now. I guess I forgot to follow up on that."

Tia stiffened when she heard this, always a little resentful of Claire sharing her sleuthing activities with anyone but herself, even though she had very little time to help out. "If you bring me the phone and the log-in info, I'll do it," she said, wanting to find some way to be included.

"I don't think I can do that," Claire said, "but I'll go through the numbers with Jason, his brother-in-law, to see if he knows anything and then maybe I can bring you some of the numbers to follow up. Thanks, Tia."

Tia nodded stiffly, and it was clear that she felt slightly miffed.

Claire sighed. She longed for the good old days when she and Tia could immerse themselves fully in a case and muddle through it together, including whatever hair-raising adventures it led to. But the recent twists and turns in their lives had laid bare the differences between them. Claire was still willing to compromise and work around her various domestic issues in order to track a killer to the ground, but Tia had different priorities and her priorities came first.

Even if Claire had been able to sway Tia to run with her head-first into this latest adventure, she would never have been able to work around Jimmy. He was firmly convinced that Tia belonged entirely to him and Mario and Marion and the house. Whatever was left over, she needed to spend on her job but certainly not on Claire with her wild ways.

Tia had prepared a lunch for them and after that the three children had a nap but then it was time to leave. It had been a lovely day, Claire thought sadly, but it wasn't like the old days.

Back at home, Claire dealt with the twins and Jessie and supper and the evening routine, and a brief half hour relaxing with Dan, before they were both so tired that they had to go to bed. But while Dan was getting ready for bed, Claire crept back out to the living room and made a quick phone call to Jason. They set a time to get together and go through whatever information was on Stefano's phone and for Claire to borrow the family phone book.

# - 24 -

## The Clue in the Phone Book

The next morning, Claire woke up with renewed purpose in regard to the investigation. As soon as she'd dealt with her morning domestic duties, she called Jason and arranged to meet him at his office that afternoon. Dan was home that day and when Claire put the twins down for their afternoon nap, he agreed to watch them so Claire could slip out for an hour to meet with Jason.

Claire arrived a few minutes early for her appointment with him at his office. Jason had picked up the phone and the two phone books from the house the night before and brought them with him. "Like I told you, Claire, the police were unable to get into Jason's phone because they didn't have the code, so I don't know how it's going to help you."

"I saw something in the old book when I was at the house searching it and I just wanted to follow up," she replied, rapidly sifting through the pages. "Ah, here it is." Claire was looking at a series of four numbers lightly recorded in pencil at the bottom of the second to last page. There was nothing to indicate what they stood for or why they were there.

Claire picked up Jason's phone and entered the number, but nothing happened. Just then Jason's secretary called to inform him that his next client was waiting. "I'll phone you tonight after I go through everything," Claire replied, heading towards the door. Jason looked after her as if he'd like to know more, but he knew his next client was the type to become very impatient if kept waiting.

By the time Claire returned home, both of the twins were up and Dan was doing his best to cope. Claire swung immediately into mother mode and it wasn't until ten o'clock that evening that she had time to experiment with Jason's phone. She turned to the four numbers she'd found at the back of the phone book. Claire had hope for these because she herself sometimes wrote down phone numbers or passwords without remembering to indicate what they were for. She thought it possible that Stefano might have done the same thing in this case. And then there was always the possibility that it had been deliberate to prevent Mona from knowing the code.

Claire entered the numbers again into the phone just in case she'd misarranged them the first time, but nothing happened. Then she entered them in reverse order. Still nothing. She thought back to what she'd learned from Matthew, Amanda's grandson, now in his third year of computer studies at the University of Alberta, and she fiddled around with the phone some more. Still nothing. Yet Claire had a strong feeling that those numbers were important. But regretfully she had to give up for the night as Dan had just come into the bedroom to get ready for bed.

The next day was Wednesday and Bethany arrived at nine and would stay until three. Claire decided that the best way she could spend the day was to get in touch with Sid Cyber's wife. She checked the entry in Stefano and Mona's phone book. There it was: Cyber, Fam——just as Jason had described it. Claire peered at it for a while and then let her eyes roam over the rest of the page.

*What's different about it?* she asked herself. And then she knew. The writing was different. The rest of the items were entered in Mona's rather childlike style, reminiscent of the handwriting of students in upper elementary grades. But this writing was scrawled in a sloped and definitive manner, obviously written by someone who had no doubts about their handwriting.

Claire went to a bedroom drawer and retrieved a magnifying glass in order to study the entry more closely. Once it was enlarged and under a strong light, she could see that the 'Fam' was unclear. It could just as easily be four letters instead of three. She picked up the phone and dialed the number, hoping that Sid Cyber would have left for work and she'd have a chance to talk to his wife.

"Hello," came a tentative female voice. "Who's calling, please?"

"Hello. Is this Mrs. Cyber?"

"Yes, this is Fran Cyber. How can I help you?"

Claire grinned to herself. So that's what the entry really said. "This is Claire Burke speaking. I'm a friend of Rosetta de Felice, Mona Amato's mother. She's asked me to look into the death of Mona and Stefano. I'm sure you must have read about their murder in the papers."

"Y-e-s, but I don't see how I can help you. It has nothing to do with me."

"Well, I did find your number in their phone book, recorded in Stefano's handwriting. There must be some reason for that. Perhaps I should ask your husband."

"No. Please don't do that. Look, can we meet? I'm home today. Could you come over here?"

Claire collected Fran's address and arranged to meet with her at eleven that morning. Smiling to herself smugly she hurried to get ready. As it turned out, the Cyber house was quite close to Rosetta's home, only a few blocks to the east and on the same street, so Claire had no difficulty finding it. It looked neat and tidy enough from the front and she climbed the steps hoping that she'd finally get some answers, or at least a better idea of where to look.

It was not to be as simple as all that, however.

# - 25 -

## Two Surprise Meetings

Claire rang the bell, and the door opened with a jerk. She was startled to see a man standing there instead of the woman she was expecting to meet. He looked at her calculatingly with cold eyes, and then stepped back from the door and motioned her in.

Claire stepped in slowly and said, "I was hoping to speak to Mrs. Cyber. I found her name written in Stefano and Mona Amato's phone book and I thought she might be able to give me some information. I'm searching for their killer."

"Yes, she told me——but I'm afraid she's somewhat indisposed at the moment," he drawled. Claire felt cold chills go down her back. "I think I know what this is about, and I can help you however," he added, and motioned to a chair in the adjoining living room after first staring pointedly at her shoes.

Claire was unsure what to do. She felt warning signals clanging inside her head and knew that without her shoes, she increased her risk of being able to escape quickly if necessary. However, her urge for answers won out and she meekly removed them and sat down as directed.

"Before we start talking," Sid Cyber instructed in a cold

voice, I'd like you to open your purse so that I can make sure you're not taping our conversation." Claire opened her purse and passed it to him. It seemed the wisest thing to do.

"He checked it quickly and handed it back, asking her what she'd like to know.

"Well, I believe you already talked to Mona's brother-in-law, Jason Albright, but he said that you had no information about Mona and Stefano, and that you didn't even know them."

"Well, that's not entirely true. I never met either of them directly, but I certainly knew of them, particularly of this Stefano character." After a pause, he added, "And of course my wife knew him——too well, I might add."

"She did?" Claire bleated weakly, gazing in awe at the cold anger on his face.

"Oh, yes. He roped her in pretty handily. My wife has had so-called 'mental health problems' for years so I imagine she was an easy catch. But she's paying for it now. And he paid, too——got what he deserved. Only trouble is he didn't live long enough to suffer the way I wanted him to."

Claire rose to her feet in horror, babbling words that hardly made sense. "Well, it was nice meeting you, Mr. Cyber. Thanks for the information. I'll be on my way now."

"I don't think so," he said, grabbing her by the shoulder.

Claire plopped back down in the chair and looked at him imploringly. "I'm just a mother with twin babies at home. I met Mona at a mother-baby group. I want to clear her name. I don't believe she killed her husband. That's all I want," she added in a quavering voice.

"That fat bitch! She tried to stop me when I was busy dishing out justice. I guess I showed her how much that meant to me."

"Okay, maybe you thought you had a right. You got away with it so far so maybe your luck will hold. You don't have to worry about me. I'll just go and stop bothering you."

"No, I'm afraid you know too much. That bastard took

enough from me already. I'm not going to jail for something he had coming to him."

Claire cowered in her chair wondering what would happen next. But just then the doorbell rang, and there was a fierce pounding on the door. Suddenly, a disheveled-looking woman ran from the back of the house and tried to get the door open. She had almost succeeded before Sid stopped her, wrenching her arms back until she screamed.

"Stand back," came the command from the other side of the door, and suddenly there was a fierce jolt and the door flew inward, accompanied by the sound of splintering wood.

Claire was so dazed she didn't even recognize them at first. But then she did. "Don!" she exclaimed. "What are you doing here?"

"I told you before, I have you flagged. A call came in stating that you were here and were in danger. I was notified. Fortunately, Al and I were nearby."

Claire looked over his shoulder and saw that Sergeant Al Crombie had quickly and efficiently placed Sid in handcuffs. He didn't look so intimidating now with two strong policemen in the room.

Having satisfied himself that Claire was all right, Don turned his attention to the woman who'd made the call, Sid's wife, Fran. "That's a nasty eye you've got there," he commented. "Do you want to press charges?"

Fran looked at her husband nervously. "Oh, no, no. It's my fault... a cupboard door. Inspector Don McCoy inspected her eye carefully, noting the circular gash on the skin beside it. Then he walked behind Sid and examined his hands, paying particular attention to the ring with the large stone in it on his right hand. "I don't think so," he said. "Not unless your cupboard has a ring on its corner."

Sergeant Crombie took charge then, and Claire observed to herself that this was something he'd been doing with increasing frequency during their recent shared cases.

"I think we'd better all sit down now so we can discuss what just happened here." Claire noticed that Sid wasn't demanding that they take their shoes off, although they'd made a point of carefully wiping them on the mat once he was in handcuffs and Don McCoy had satisfied himself that Claire was all right.

"I think you'd better start, Claire. What brought you here?"

# - 26 -
## Another Kind of Crime

Claire sat back in her chair and tried to pull her thoughts together. *How am I going to be able to give Inspector McCoy and Sergeant Crombie a satisfactory explanation for my involvement in this affair?* she asked herself. But then she remembered the answer. It wasn't as if she could be accused of interfering with a police investigation this time. There was no investigation. It had been shut down, very prematurely in her opinion. *I have nothing to apologize for. In fact, I've been performing a public service,* she told herself and began.

"An acquaintance of mine was murdered along with her husband, and the inspector in charge of the case dismissed it as a murder-suicide after only a very perfunctory review of the evidence at the scene. I have reason to believe that their conclusion was in error and have been searching for the real answer along with some interested others."

"That would be the Amato case, I expect," McCoy commented.

"Yes," Claire said in surprise. "How did you know?"

"Humph, was all he said. But the disgusted look on his face

told Claire much more.

"Go on, Claire," Al said evenly.

"I've interviewed Mona's mother and her sister and her sister's husband and Stefano's brother and his wife. Every one of them believes this is not something Mona could have done. She just didn't have that kind of energy or initiative. She was kind of depressed and inert."

"You have to have 'initiative' to commit murder now?" McCoy asked sarcastically.

Claire opened her mouth to respond but Sergeant Crombie again took over. "That doesn't explain why you're here. What involvement does this man have in all this?"

"We found his name in their family phonebook and have been reaching out to all the entries there."

"Woah. Back up a bit. Who's 'we'?"

"Mostly Mona's sister's husband and a colleague of Stefano and that colleague's wife. We've joined together because we want justice for Mona. Oh," she added as an afterthought, "and I've been running things by Tia, of course. We always work together on these cases, as you know, but she's too busy to actively participate this time."

McCoy couldn't help sniffing when he heard this, even though he was secretly pleased that Claire had involved herself in the case because he'd not been at all satisfied with the way the new inspector had described to him and the other unit members how he'd resolved it. He started to say something, but Sergeant Crombie interrupted again. "Why was your name in the phonebook?" he asked, turning to Sid.

"It wasn't my name. It was her name," he said, pointing at his wife who was huddling in a far corner of the room. "Why don't you ask her?"

"We'll get to that," McCoy interjected. "What I want to know right now is what was going on here when we arrived? Why were we even called?"

"This man as much as admitted to me that he killed them," Claire exclaimed. "That's why he wouldn't let me leave and God knows what he was planning to do to me." She looked with horror at Fran's rapidly swelling eye and the still-oozing gash beside it.

"I did no such thing!" Sid yelled, jumping to his feet. "She's a liar!"

"You told me!" Claire began.

McCoy cut her off and turned to Fran. "Do you know anything about this, ma'am?"

Fran looked miserable and gazed furtively at her husband. "I, I …I don't think it was murder."

"What was it then?" Sergeant McCoy asked in a patient voice, obviously trying to de-escalate the rising tension in the room.

"It was, it was…about the car." She turned to her husband. "Tell them, Sid," she pleaded. "You don't want them thinking it's murder."

"I want a lawyer," he snarled.

Inspector McCoy took over at that point. He turned to Sid. "I'm arresting you on a charge of uttering threats and possible domestic abuse with further possible charges pending."

He turned to Sergeant McCoy then and asked him to call in the waiting police officers. Then he faced Claire. "You'll have to come to the station and complete a statement of what happened during your visit here." Finally, he turned to Fran. "I recommend you get that eye seen to at an emergency room. It looks pretty bad to me. We can drive you there if you wish."

But Fran just shook her head. "I've had worse," was all she said. But, after Sid was taken away, she added, "I suggest you look in the Amato garage if you want to know what Sid did."

At the station, Claire tried her best to recall Sid's exact words but she couldn't quite capture them. In truth, she'd been too frightened to even process clearly when he was speaking. Sergeant Crombie read over her work and questioned her further on exactly what she'd heard. "Did he ever say he killed them or murdered them or got rid of them? What made you think he was referring to doing them bodily harm?"

They'd been at it for about half an hour when the door opened, and Inspector McCoy came in. He'd gone immediately to the Amato garage. Jason had met him there to open it up, thanks to Claire's call to him at the office. "Stefano's car, a new silver Prius, has been rammed and severely damaged on the front and right side, chrome crumpled light knocked out, fender bashed in. Do you think that might have been what Sid was talking about, Claire?"

Claire sat there stunned for a minute. Then, all of a sudden, some pieces fell into place. "That must be what he meant when he said he wished he could have made Stefano suffer more for what he did. He must have meant that he never lived to see the damage to his car. It must have happened when it was parked there, maybe on the street."

"That would make sense," McCoy said. "In its present condition nobody would've been able to drive it more than a short distance. The fender was caved in right against the wheel."

"But then who put it in the garage? Did Sid do it after he killed them?"

"But why do that to the car if he was going to kill them anyway?" Sergeant Crombie asked.

"If he killed them," Claire said slowly. "When I think back on what he said, I'm pretty sure everything could fit with just doing the damage to the car. But he said something about Mona trying to stop him. She must have been home at the time. Maybe Mona put the car in the garage. "No," she went on. I remember when Mona spoke at the mother-baby group where I met her. She said she couldn't drive." She would probably have just called Stefano and asked him to come home to deal with the situation. Something else must have happened that day. Maybe somebody else was lurking around——the real killer."

Inspector McCoy had listened with uncharacteristic patience

to Claire's mental wanderings. By this time, he knew better than to dismiss her thoughts out of hand, however weird they might sound. She'd been right too often. But when she finished talking, he simply said, "I think it's time you went home, Claire." He could see how tired she was. "You brought your own car here, right?"

She looked at him. "Can you take over this case, Don, since it's been officially closed?"

"I'm already working on doing that," he replied. "And don't worry. We're going out now to canvas the neighbours. A violent crash like that——somebody must have heard it. I can't believe it's not in the police report." He had that disgusted look on his face again.

"Okay, I'm going." Claire suddenly realized how exhausted, she was, a delayed reaction to her earlier trauma. "I feel better now that I know you and Al will be involved," she said.

"Oh, and Claire?" Don McCoy said sweetly.

"Yes?"

"Stay out of it. Something very ugly could have happened if we hadn't come along. And it's just by chance that that woman had the sense to call it in."

"I'll be in touch," was all Claire said as she left the room.

# - 27 -
## Yet Another New Direction

When Claire got home, Dan was scrambling to cope with all three children at once and he looked at her resentfully. "I can explain," she said wearily. "But I'll do it later. It was entirely beyond my control."

Somehow Claire found the strength to make it through the evening routine and to have a shower. But then she collapsed in bed and was asleep within seconds. Dan looked at her tenderly. He knew something had happened, but it could wait until tomorrow. Fortunately, he didn't have to go into the office until his first appointment at eleven.

After Jessie left for school the next morning and the twins were down for their morning nap, Claire and Dan sat down with their coffee for a catch-up time. Claire told him everything that had happened, and he was, of course, horrified. "Why did you agree to go to her home after the way he dealt with Jason? Why didn't you ask her to meet you somewhere else?"

"I guess I didn't think I had that much leverage with her and I better take what she was willing to offer——or I'd end up with nothing."

"And as it turns out, that would have been just fine. You said that it's very unlikely that he's the killer."

"Sure, but I didn't know that in advance. That's the way these investigations work. You only make progress by following every lead that comes along, even though most of them amount to nothing."

"Well, you're through with those people now anyway."

"Not really," Claire said. "I still didn't get a chance to talk to Fran about Stefano, and that was the whole point."

"It doesn't matter. I don't want you to go anywhere near her. You said that Inspector McCoy was getting involved. Let him handle it."

"He won't ask the right questions," Claire said, the irritation clear on her face. I have a theory."

"You always have a theory, and one of these days your theory is going to get you killed."

"Okay, I promise to leave it for now. I have another line to follow up anyway."

Dan looked at her suspiciously but said nothing. He knew it was no use. After he left and after the twins had had their morning play session following their nap and had their lunch, they went down for their second nap and Claire pulled out the notes she'd been making on the case. She found the number for Bif's Bicycle Shop and dialed it.

"Hello, Bif's Bicycle Shop. Bif speaking."

"Hello," Claire replied. "Could I please speak to Leonard Reicher?"

"Leonard? He's not here anymore. He's been gone a long time."

"Oh," Claire said, disappointed. "Do you have any idea how I could reach him?"

"Uh. Who is this?"

"Oh, sorry. My name is Claire Burke. I wanted to tell Leonard about the death of his former girlfriend. I'm looking for her killer and since they were together a long time, I thought he might know of some contacts I could follow up with."

"Are you a police officer.?"

"No, but I do consultation work for them on certain cases, cases like this where the trail has gone cold and there doesn't seem to be any answer. I've been quite lucky in finding answers for several of them."

"So you're like a private investigator?"

"Not quite. Like I said, I have a formal affiliation with the police, the detective unit."

"Uh, okay. I guess it would be okay to tell you. Leonard is working at a different bicycle shop now, a big operator. He got a position as their chief technician."

"And what's the name of this shop?"

"It's Union Cycle. He's at their south side branch on Calgary Trail."

"Do you have a number for them?"

"No, but I'm sure you can get it from the operator."

"Okay, and thanks very much." Claire hung up, fuming. By the time she found the number and called, she was quite sure Bif would have phoned Leonard and warned him about the nature of her call. She quickly found the number on the net and dialed. He answered the phone himself and she could tell by his cautious tone that he had indeed been warned and had already been busy preparing his story.

Once Claire had gone over the reason for her call, she asked Leonard, "When was the last time you saw Mona?"

"Well, the last time I actually talked to her face to face would have been almost three years ago. But I did go by her house a couple of times just to kind of check on her and see if she was okay. I may have seen her through the window once or twice."

"And when was the last time you did that?"

"Oh, I haven't done that for a couple of years now, about the time I started going out with Gail. We're together now, and we have a two-month-old baby girl. We're calling her Sharon, after

Gail's grandmother."

"I see," Claire responded, unsure where to go from there. "Er... congratulations! Uh, would you say you and Gail are happy together?"

Leonard didn't respond right away, but then he said. "That's kind of a personal question, isn't it?"

"Yes. I'm sorry. It's just that I'm looking for anything that can help me understand what happened to Mona. Did you know anyone who might want to hurt her?"

"I'd like to know that, too. Mona could be difficult at times, but she didn't deserve that. I can't think of anyone, but I could ask Gail. She used to work with her."

"She did? Could I talk to her?"

"I don't know. She's kind of busy with the baby and all. And I know she wouldn't like visitors because she can't keep the house up right now the way she likes it and she would be embarrassed." Leonard paused then but Claire said nothing. "Maybe," he added, "if you give me your phone number, I could get her to call you when she has a minute."

Claire decided to settle for that, so she thanked Leonard and ended the call. He'd asked her to let him know if she found out who killed Mona and she'd agreed. From the tenor of their phone call, Claire was quite certain that Leonard had nothing to do with it——and that was that. She had now officially run out of leads and had no idea where to go from there.

# - 28 -
## Nowhere Left to Go

Claire had hung up the phone feeling frustrated, irritable and at loose ends. But then she looked around her house and gave herself a good shake. Housework was not her favorite activity, but she decided that some vigorous cleaning might also clear the cobwebs out of her brain. Also, she was recalling, with a mixture of embarrassment and resentment, how clean and orderly Tia's house had been, even though she had an active three-year old and a full-time job to cope with, not to mention her precocious 14-year-old son and her demanding husband.

Just as Claire pulled out her Dyson vacuum cleaner, the twins began fighting over a toy and Claire sat down to redirect them, soon becoming involved in their play. A happy hour passed and then it was time to change them and feed them their dinner. After that, she'd need to prepare their own dinner as Dan would be home soon. Jessie's assistant was already in the kitchen getting Jessie's supper ready, so Claire shoved the vacuum back into a corner and carried on with her main task these days, meeting the needs of Isaac and Isabel, as she found herself increasingly referring to herself.

After supper, baths for the twins and getting them down and after Jessie was in bed and her evening assistant had departed, Claire and Dan finally sat down with cups of decaf coffee to share the events of their day. But just as Claire reached for her coffee, the phone rang, and she glanced in irritation at her watch. "Who's calling at 9:30 in the evening?" she muttered to Dan, and then answered the call none too graciously.

There was a hesitation on the other end of the line and then she heard a timid hello. "Is this Claire Burke?"

"Yes, who's calling, please?" Claire responded briskly.

"Uh, this is Gail Reicher. You talked to my husband earlier today?"

"Oh, Gail. Thanks for getting back to me," Claire responded warmly.

"Leonard said you wanted to know anything I could tell you about enemies Mona might have had?"

"Yes, anything at all you could tell me might help. I've kind of run out of leads here."

"Well, I really can't think of much. She did call me once after they broke up just to ask how he was doing and to let me know that she'd seen him cruising by her place a couple of times and once even peeping in her windows."

"Did she know at that point that you were involved with him?"

"Well, that's just it, you see. We weren't yet involved at that time. It's just that we used to double date when I was going out with some other guy. Leonard called me once a month or so after that. He was still very upset and wanted to discuss the break-up. Our relationship kind of developed from there."

"Did Mona say anything else during that earlier phone call?"

"She talked a little about this Stefano guy she was seeing."

'What about him?" Claire asked patiently, recognizing that Gail was one of those people who didn't give up information unless it was pried out of them.

"She mentioned some girl he'd been seeing before her."

"Do you know her name and how I can get hold of her?"

"Her name is Annie Kozak. She's a flight stewardess and that's how they met. It might be for WestJet, but I'm not sure about that."

"That must have been awkward for their relationship, Mona taking over with Stefano after Annie and him broke up?"

"No. According to what she heard from both Stefano and Annie, it was a mutual decision. Stefano told Mona that he'd had a lot of girlfriends in the past, but this was the first time that the break-up had been mutual instead of him breaking it off."

"Is there anything else you can tell me about Mona?"

"No, not really. From what I saw of her in the store, I wouldn't say that she was overly dedicated to her work. Kind of on the lazy side, actually. But not to the point where anyone would want to kill her——or even have grounds to fire her. She was just kind of ordinary ... except——"

"Except what?" Claire asked patiently, rolling her eyes.

"Well, I'd say she was kind of gullible, easily fooled. From what she told me about Stefano, it sounded to me like he talked a good line, a little too good to be true. I don't think he was in the same league as my Leonard."

"What made you think that?"

"I don't know. I really don't know anymore ... and the baby's crying now so I have to go."

"Okay. Well, thanks very much for calling. Bye."

Claire hung up the phone and looked at Dan who'd been listening in. "Another dead end," she said. Just maybe a little more support for the picture that's been forming about this Stefano character. And also for this picture of Mona as not very perceptive about other people."

# - 29 -

## A Possible Breakthrough

It was a Tuesday morning. Jessie had just left for school and Dan was leaving shortly for his office. Claire contemplated the vacuum sourly and wondered if that was what she should do with her copious spare time, i.e. those rare minutes not devoted to the twin's happiness and upkeep. Then she remembered that the mother-baby group was meeting that morning. She hadn't been for a while because of the murder issue and it would be nice to see everyone again.

Twins in tow, Claire set off along the now familiar road and soon she was ensconced in the loveseat in Ella's living room, one twin snuggling against her on each side. Everyone was happy to see her and anxious to hear about what progress she'd made in terms of finding the murderer of Mona and Stefano. Claire shared freely since she didn't see how it could do any harm and also since she wasn't bound by a confidentiality agreement with any employer. When she finally finished, Valerie was quick to ask a question.

"You mentioned this Annie person who previously broke up with Stefano. Are you going to follow up on that?"

"Yes, if I can find her."

Delsie, another mother, spoke up then. "I have a friend who's a flight attendant for WestJet. I could find out if she knows this Annie Kozak. Or even if she doesn't, maybe she might know how to find out. Maybe there's a list of flight attendants or maybe even some professional group they all belong to."

"That would be great, Delsie. I wasn't looking forward to even trying because I know the airline wouldn't share any staff information with me." The rest of the session passed pleasantly. Unfortunately, Mona's mother Rosetta had never taken up Claire's suggestion to join the group. Claire knew she was still grieving heavily and asking herself again and again if this would've happened if things had been different——if Mona would have even married Stefano.

Claire was enjoying the group experience so much that she didn't want it to end and after it was over, she invited Valerie and her son, Jeffrey, home for lunch, completely forgetting her recent promise to herself never to do that again in the foreseeable future. However, she knew Valerie wouldn't mind a little dust and Jeffrey, although five months older than the twins, seemed to play nicely with them.

Valerie accepted happily and they chatted away as they walked back to Claire's house, but part of Claire's mind was occupied in reviewing the supplies in the fridge and calculating what to do with what was available. She decided that a quick pasta dish would have to do, recalling that there was a half jar of Costco pesto sauce in the fridge that really needed to be used up. There were also some odd bits of leftover vegetables: a couple of stocks of Swiss Chard, some Bok Choy and a little Gai Choy as well. And there were a few sprigs of leftover parsley just hanging on.

Once back at the house, the baby changing ceremony began. Then it was time for Isabel to be nursed and Valerie gave Isaac his bottle at the same time. Jeffrey was content to sit beside them with his glass of juice in hand. He no longer drank from a bottle. Meanwhile, Claire had managed to get the pasta water on and after Isabel finished nursing, she switched to Isaac for a few minutes and then left the children with Valerie.

Back in the kitchen, Claire washed, trimmed and diced the vegetables together finely in her food processor. Then she microwaved them for one minute, quickly wiping down and setting the table in the interim before the buzzer rang. When the water boiled, she added the pasta and some salt, stirred the pot and turned the heat to medium. Claire got out the colander and placed a bowl inside. This was to catch some of the water in case she needed to thin the pasta sauce or to use it to bring Jessie's meals to the right consistency when she ground whatever they didn't use today for future lunches for dinners for her. She placed the cheese and grater on the table and then quickly drained the pasta.

Claire was so used to this kind of multi-tasking that she didn't even think twice about it, but Valerie sat back and watched her in amazement. "I sure wish I was as efficient as you in the kitchen," Valerie commented.

"Well, I wish I was half as good a housekeeper as my friend, Tia——but cleaning just doesn't interest me as much as cooking."

"My thought is that if we don't all want to go crazy with guilt over our inadequacies, then we all ought to just follow our strengths——go where we shine and ignore the rest," Valerie declared emphatically.

Claire laughed heartily at this bit of homespun philosophical rationalization and thought once again how comfortable it was to be around Valerie. But as she was thinking, she was also multi-tasking——dishing the penne into three little bowls and sprinkling cheese on top. She stopped before adding it to Jeffrey's dish, aware of how picky children could be. "Does Jeffrey like Parmesan?"

"Better not add any to his dish. His tastes are quite fickle, and I can never tell from one day to the next what he'll tolerate and what he won't. But if you have any Velveeta or mild cheddar cheese slices, I know he'd love that."

"I'm sorry but I don't," Claire said, deciding not to share her opinion on the subject of processed cheese.

"Okay, well, he'll be fine with the plain pasta and pesto then. Don't worry about it," Val replied. But Claire was already thinking. She grabbed a package of shredded mozzarella from her freezer, sprinkled some on top of Jeffrey's dish and popped it in the microwave for 20 seconds, just until it began to melt nicely on top. Then she stirred it gently to mix it in but not completely, licked the spoon to make sure it was not too hot and handed it to Jeffrey with a clean spoon.

Jeffrey looked at the dish, looked at his mother and began to eat with gusto. Valerie rolled her eyes and laughed. He never attacks my food that enthusiastically. Maybe I'll buy some shredded mozzarella."

"Just keep it in the freezer. Then it'll always be there when you need it. I always keep an extra bottle of pesto Sauce in the freezer as well. Since it's not cooked and therefore not sterile, it must always be refrigerated and still has quite a limited shelf life. Oh! And I also keep packages of frozen chopped spinach in the freezer. Then on those lazy days or the days when I don't have leftover vegetables to use up, I just substitute a pack of spinach for the extra vegetables in the pesto sauce."

"Do you ever use just plain pesto sauce?"

Claire nodded. "Sometimes, just for Dan and me. It's delicious that way and much more authentically Italian——but not nearly as nutritious." Claire was fairly obsessed with nutrition and loved to tweak recipes to maximize their nutritional value, sometimes quite successfully and other times not so much.

The meal proceeded happily, and they finished off with a bowl of green grapes, the ones for the children carefully cut into quarters so they wouldn't choke on them. After that, there was more baby changing, bottles, nursing, et cetera, until finally all three children graciously decided to nap and Claire and Valerie enjoyed the luxury of a little adult to adult time.

When Dan came home that evening, he was relieved to find Claire in a cheerful mood and she told him all about her day when they finally had their sit-down time together. But the moment was slightly chillèd when the phone rang, and it was Delsie with news. "I talked to my friend, and she knew exactly who I meant. In fact, she's been on a few flights with Annie and even had her phone number. She rang her up and got permission for me to give it to you. Have you got a pen and paper handy?"

Claire grabbed some paper, wrote down the number, thanked Delsie fulsomely and hung up the phone. She turned to Dan with a big smile. "This is great. Delsie said that this Annie had actually kept in touch with Stefano and knows something about his other associates. Maybe I'll finally get some new leads to follow."

"Goody," Dan said glumly. "Just remember what I said about not taking any more chances. And since Inspector McCoy made the effort to take over somebody else's case, it would seem that the only right thing to do is to hand over any new leads to him. He is, after all, the one being paid to put himself in dangerous situations."

"Humph," Claire said. But then she thought she'd better do something to reassure Dan. "I can promise you that I will only be meeting people in public places from now on," she said. "Besides, I don't have permission to give this information to the police, so I pretty well have to follow it up myself. She said good-night then and went off to get ready for bed, humming to herself, recalling as she did that the next day was Wednesday, Bethany's day, which meant that she was free to pursue her own interests. *Hopefully, Dan will be going into the office,* she thought to herself. And then her head hit the pillow and she was asleep.

# - 30 -
## Now or Never

The next day, Claire went through the morning routine on autopilot and after Jessie and Dan left and Bethany arrived to take over, she sat down with the phone to call Annie. They arranged to meet for lunch as it was one of Annie's days off and settled on a nice restaurant a short car ride from Claire's house. Claire spent a leisurely hour getting ready and skipped out of the house in a positive frame of mind. Today was going to be the day. She just knew it.

At 11:30, Claire arrived at Aristocrats, a new Italian restaurant in the southwest part of Edmonton. She was fifteen minutes early and used the time to search out the most private booth she could find there. Satisfied, she sat down and when the server arrived, she checked out the menu and ordered unsweetened iced tea. The menu advertised free refills, and she asked for some extra lemon slices and pulled a small bag of Stevia out of her purse. Claire had done well on her diet over the past couple of years, even with the birth of the twins, and she didn't want to slide backward.

Annie Kozak arrived a few minutes later, and after brief introductions, they quickly ordered their food and got down to business. "How well did you know Stefano?" Claire asked.

"Pretty well. Probably better than most."

"What does that mean? You said you had an affair with him. Was it still ongoing when he died?"

"Oh, no. In fact, it wasn't really an affair. We just hooked up a few times."

"I don't understand," Claire replied.

"Stef and I met when we were both at a low point in our lives. We weren't really all that attracted to each other, but we started sleeping together anyway, more for something to do than anything else. Then I met somebody I really was attracted to and I terminated my arrangement with Stefano but not our friendship."

Claire tried not to look shocked. "Why did you want the friendship to continue?" she asked.

"I was intrigued by him. He treated me like 'one of the guys'. Only it was pretty obvious by the way he talked that he never would have been one of the guys himself. He was trying too hard, kind of posturing one might say. He talked to me about all the girls he'd been with, but it was almost like he wanted to know if he'd passed some test or other."

"I still don't understand why you kept the relationship going. You don't make him sound like good friend material exactly."

"I guess I felt sorry for him and maybe I thought I could help him somehow. He seemed kind of pathetic to me."

"What about his relationship with his wife? Why do you suppose he even spent time and energy going after other women if he already had a wife and baby daughter at home?"

Annie looked pensive for a moment. Finally, she said, "I think he was trying to prove something to himself. I noticed that every time he started a new relationship, he got this energy going, stood up taller, looked prouder somehow."

"Yes, that fits with what I've already heard," Claire replied, and she shared a little of what Stefano's brother, Marco, had told her about his early life.

"What about Stefano's wife? Do you think Mona knew about his affairs?"

"I don't know but she must have at least suspected. You can only 'work late at the office' so many times before it starts to sound fishy."

"Did he talk to you about his relationship with her?"

"He complained that she was very needy and demanding—and on the lazy side. He said she was always trying to palm off caring for the baby on him when he was at home."

"Do you think he talked about her to the women he dated?"

"Definitely. I think he made them feel sorry for him, like they had to make it up to him, somehow. I'm pretty sure that's how he got them into bed with him. It wasn't his charm and his 'clever' moves, because from what I experienced with him, those were pretty staged and clichéd."

"Do you think the marriage would have lasted if he and Mona hadn't been killed?"

"You know, it's funny that you're asking that. Towards the end, in our talks together I felt like he was reflecting more and more on his life and growing up a bit. Especially when we'd been drinking together pretty heavily, he'd start talking about Mona. A couple of times he mentioned that she was the only one who really knew him deep down and accepted him for who he was. From what he said it sounded like they'd had some good talks together in those few months and that she was beginning to mature also."

"Why do you suppose they ever got together in the first place? She didn't seem to have that much going for her from the one time I met her."

"From what Stefano told me about her I think she was probably just as broken as him. Maybe they saw a way that they could fit their jagged edges together and make a whole life ... something like that."

Annie looked slightly embarrassed by her poetic speech, but

Claire just nodded soberly. "That actually fits with what I've managed to cobble together from the bits I've picked up about both of them. Although I found Mona highly irritating on the one occasion when I met her, there were moments when something else in her seemed to be peeking out from beneath her surface. I suspect she had experienced a lot of hurt in her life one way or another." Claire thought for a moment about whether or not to reveal the alcoholism Rosetta had speculated about Mona's mother and then decided to go ahead, explaining to Annie how that might have affected her behavior and become like a form of self-sabotage hiding any good that was underneath.

Annie breathed in so deeply that Claire heard her. "That explains a lot," she replied, and Claire saw the shine of tears in her eyes.

"Okay," Claire said briskly, aware of time passing. "What you've told me has helped a lot to form a complete picture, but it still doesn't bring me any closer to finding out who the murderer was. I've already eliminated from the suspect list a lot of people in Stefano's business and personal life and in Mona's life as well, so I really have no other leads to track down at this point. It seems to me now that the most likely possibility is that it must either be someone with whom he had one of these affairs, or else somebody closely connected to them like a husband or boyfriend."

"That makes sense," Annie said slowly. "I'm trying to recall anything Stefano might have said that would point to one or another of them."

"Also, the times when these affairs took place. That would be helpful," Claire said.

"Well, I only really know about the ones that happened since I met him and maybe not even all of those, although it seems pretty likely. Stefano didn't pass up any opportunities to crow about them to me."

"Lovely," Claire muttered sarcastically.

"I remember him talking about an Eileen. That was some time

last year. And before her there was a Gloria. He did say that her husband found out and got pretty riled up. But you'd think if he was going to try to get even with Stefano, he'd have done it before now. The only other one I can think of is Lucy. I remember he said that she worked at Target at West Edmonton Mall. But they've shut down that store now, and I think they shut down all their stores in Canada. They're an American outfit."

"Anything else you can think of that might help?" Claire asked.

Annie sat back for a moment, reflecting. Finally, she said, "Once when we were drinking pretty heavily, he told me about somebody called Marta. He said she was his first and they were both pretty young at the time. She hung herself, he said——a little while after he ended their affair. He seemed to feel pretty badly about that. He told me she only had her father, and Stefano had heard from somebody else who knew them at the time that the father had become an alcoholic afterwards and eventually lost his job."

Claire just pursed her lips and said nothing. There was nothing to say. It was all too horribly sad to contemplate. Finally, she reached a conclusion in her head and let out a big sigh. "I think that tracking these women down is something I'm going to have to leave to my police contact. I'm going to give him a summary of the information you've given me but then he's going to need to talk to you. Will you be okay with that?"

"I don't know," Annie said warily." I don't like dealing with the police."

"Do you want Stefano and Mona's murderer to get away or do you think the conclusion the inspector who handled the case reached, that Mona was the murderer, is correct?"

"No, I can't really see that——and yes, I guess I want them to have some justice. Stefano was kind of mixed up, but I don't think that deep down he was really a bad person, just confused."

"Okay, can I contact Inspector McCoy then and share what

you told me with him?"

"I guess."

# - 31 -

## Claire Resorts to Trickery

The next morning after Dan and Jessie had left and the twins were napping, Claire called Inspector McCoy. The first thing he said to her after their initial greeting was "That material that Jason Albright picked up from the police station last week? We're going to need it back. Sergeant Crombie contacted him this morning to make arrangements and he said that you're in possession of Stefano's phone. I'm sending somebody by this morning to pick it up. Will you be home?"

Claire sighed in frustration. She'd been hoping to have more time to work at cracking the code, but she knew there was no point in arguing. "I'll be here," she said as mildly as she could.

"Good," McCoy replied briskly, sounding somewhat warmer now that he knew he could get what he wanted without an argument. "Why were you calling this morning, Claire? Have you found out anything new?"

"As a matter of fact, yes. I was able to trace down a former girlfriend of Stefano who maintained contact with him and knew something of his affairs with other women."

"That sounds odd. What …"

"It was odd, but I think you'd better talk to her yourself. Her name is Annie Kozak," and Claire gave him the phone number. "She mentioned the first names of three women with whom Stefano had affairs over the past several years, but she wasn't able to give me much useful background information on them. Perhaps you'll be able to get more out of her than I did."

Normally, Claire would've gone into more detail and tried harder to involve herself directly in the investigation. But a thought was beginning to form in the back of her mind, a loose end that needed following up and a possible way to do that. And this was not information she wanted to share with Don McCoy.

Inspector McCoy must have sensed something off in their interaction, the unexpected helpfulness and lack of pushiness on Claire's part, for he confronted her on it. "Is there anything else, Claire? Anything you're not telling me? You seem anxious to end this conversation."

"No. No. It's just, uh——I hear Isaac waking up and I better get to him."

He couldn't argue with that and before they ended the call, McCoy reminded her once more that someone would be by to pick up the phone. Claire then checked on the twins, but they were both still sleeping. She picked up Stefano's phone and spent several minutes trying to figure out the code without success. Soon, however, she was interrupted by sounds from the bedroom and her mothering day began again. But a plan was formulating in her mind.

The next morning, a Friday, Claire managed to find a few minutes to call two schools. At the first one, she inquired about some dates, and at the second, she inquired about the possibility of accessing some school yearbooks from particular years. "Oh, I can just look that up for you," the helpful receptionist replied. "Just tell me the last name of the girl you're searching for."

This didn't suit Claire's purposes at all, and she quickly made up a story that she hoped would be believable. "Well, that's just it you see. We don't know. Her mother——that's my sister, Marie——

–had custody after the divorce but her daughter, Rose, was kidnapped five years ago by the father. They were living in Toronto at the time and Marie hired a detective to track them down. He got a lead on the father and then traced him as far as the Pleasant View area here in Edmonton, but he couldn't narrow it down any further than that. Rose isn't registered with either school board in the city, and we think he may have legally changed his name and hers and that's why we can't find her. But if I could just look at the pictures, I'm pretty sure I'd recognize her."

"Well, even if we could allow that, wouldn't it be better for her mother to examine the yearbook pictures? It's her daughter, after all."

"Yes, that would be best. But Marie has been so worn down by all this that she's actually ended up in hospital. If by some miracle I could find Rose, I know that that would be the tonic she needed, and she'd snap out of whatever spell she seems to be under. Could I please just come and look? I have a strong feeling this could be it. Her father was an ardent Catholic when I knew him with very strong views on keeping his daughter in a religious context. And yours is the only Catholic high school in the area. Please. It would mean so much to my poor sister if I could finally locate her daughter, her only child."

"I don't know if that's okay or not and the principal isn't here today. She's away at a conference in another city. But she'll be back on Monday and I could ask her then. Could you wait until Monday?"

"Not really. My sister may not even be alive by then. She won't eat, and she's going down every day. She's just lost her will to live."

*I hope I'm not laying it on too thick,* Claire said to herself, but then she heard a half-sob on the other end of the phone line. "Oh, this is such a sad situation. Just come and I'll explain to the principal on Monday how important it was."

"Thank you. I'll be there in an hour," Claire replied. She hung up the phone and frantically phoned Bethany to beg her to take over with the twins for the rest of the morning.

"I just pulled everything out of my kitchen cupboards. I can't leave this mess here. Daryl will be home at three and he'll expect to find the house in order," she replied primly.

"Look, Bethany. Just come over. This is really important. I'll go back to your place with the twins and help you when I get back. I promise."

Bethany agreed grudgingly and arrived just ten minutes later since she only lived a short distance away. Claire gave her some last-minute instructions and rushed out the door.

At the school, the receptionist was ready for her. "I have pulled the yearbooks for the years you wanted and set them up in a small room off the gym. Come along and I'll show you."

Claire trotted along beside her and soon she was settled in a private, quiet space with the yearbooks. *Perfect,* she said to herself. *Nobody can see what I am really looking for.* Twenty minutes later she found it. Then she went more closely over the yearbook and identified the same girl in a couple of group pictures. Claire took snaps with her phone and wrote down any information that could possibly be helpful. Satisfied, she picked up the books and returned to the receptionist's desk.

"Did you find her?" the receptionist asked eagerly.

"Yes, I think I did——but now I need an address."

"Tell me who it is and which years she was in school here. I'll look it up on our registration lists."

"Well, that's the problem. I didn't fully explain myself before but actually I'm an official consultant to the police. And this is a delicate matter that requires the utmost privacy.

"I can't share this information with anyone but them, and time is of the essence as I said. Is there any way you could just show me the grade eleven class registration list for 2015? I know you have to keep student addresses on file."

"Oooh. I don't know about that. All our information here is

confidential and I have a bad feeling that I've already breached that confidentiality by giving you access to the yearbooks. I just figured that if students already have copies then a lot of people have access to them so what's the harm? But this is different. Giving out student addresses——that really is going too far."

"I was afraid of that," Claire sighed. "I guess I'll just have to phone Inspector McCoy and explain what I've found out and ask him to get a search warrant ready to deliver to your principal when she returns on Monday. I just hope my sister makes it. I'll call McCoy right now and then I'll visit her and tell her there's hope." Claire picked up her phone.

"The receptionist looked relieved at first, then confused and finally fearful. "No, you can't do that," she begged, placing a restraining hand on Claire's arm. "Then Principal Higgins will know that I let you look at the yearbooks."

Claire said nothing but just looked at her questioningly.

"Okay," the receptionist decided. "I'm going to get that list out and leave it in my top desk drawer. Then I'm going to the bathroom. I'm a diabetic and I need to give myself an insulin shot at this time of day, so it'll take me a few minutes. I think we've finished our business so why don't you leave now? I really can't leave my desk if anyone is in the office."

Claire turned and walked out the door. She waited a couple of minutes in the hall and then re-entered the office, walking directly to the bank of drawers at the back of the outward facing desk. She found the document and briskly walked back to the little room she'd previously occupied so she could have some privacy. It took Claire less than a minute to locate the address she needed and to copy it down. Then she rolled the document up, glanced out the door to make sure nobody was in the office and walked back to the receptionist's desk as quickly as she could. The receptionist was not back yet, so Claire hastily thrust the registration list in the drawer and walked out of the room and out of the school.

Once back at home, she was gratified to see that Bethany was in the middle of feeding the twins. Claire quickly made sandwiches for herself and Bethany and poured two glasses of juice mixed with mineral water. Then she took over with feeding Isaac while Bethany carried on in her battle of wits with Isabel who kept trying to grab the spoon. They worked together in harmony and soon the twins were fed and changed, Claire and Bethany had consumed their sandwiches and juice, a bag had been packed with essential items for the twins, including some distracting toys, and they were on their way back to Bethany's house.

Isaac and Isabel were happy to crawl around on the floor exploring a new place and Claire and Bethany got right to work. One glance around the kitchen made Claire aware of the immensity of the task.

"Don't worry," Bethany said. "At least half of this stuff is going to Goodwill."

"Well, I wouldn't know how to help you with that, and I personally hate giving stuff away when I don't know who's going to get it. I bet a lot of the best stuff in their stores is bought up by people who don't really need it. They just want a bargain."

Bethany didn't reply directly but instead asked Claire if she'd take over with washing the cupboards while Bethany did the sorting. Claire agreed and then the serious work started. After they had a lot of items sorted into boxes or back into the clean cupboards, Bethany called for a break. Claire washed her hands and happily sat down to nurse Isabel and give Isaac his bottle. Once that was done and the twins were changed and drifting off to sleep on a quilt on the floor, Bethany went to the kitchen and returned with coffee and a small glass of Grand Marnier for each of them. "I think we deserve this after all our hard work," she said.

"I agree!" Claire said, sipping her drink appreciatively.

"We've got the worst of it done, and I can finish up on my own if you want to go home now."

Claire glanced at the children and saw that they'd both drifted off to sleep. "I guess we'll be good for another half-hour. I'll take them home when they wake up."

"Great," Bethany said, and sat back sipping her coffee. "Have you ever listened to Marie Kondo or seen any of her shows?" she asked.

"I saw part of one of her shows on TV, but that sort of stuff isn't really my thing," Claire responded. "I'm not into super housewifery."

"It's not about that at all," Bethany objected. "It's about freeing yourself from excess possessions so you can use your energy to deal with the important things in your life."

Claire looked at her in surprise. Up to this time their relationship had been purely a business matter. Bethany wanted a few part-time hours of work here and there and Claire needed occasional help with the twins. She hadn't realized that Bethany held such strong views on domestic issues. "Well, I have two problems with that," Claire responded. "First, it would take me way more emotional and physical energy to figure out which of my excess possessions I could bear to part with than it would to just leave them piled in closets and stacked in the basement. Second, like I said, I'd hate for the good things I give away to go to people who don't need them but just want a bargain. Now if by some magic people would materialize on my doorstep who were really in need, I'd actually be able to give away a lot of things quite happily and I wouldn't mind the work involved. It would feel like a real accomplishment then. But just dumping it with some charitable organization that does God knows what with it does not."

"I don't agree with your reasoning, Claire. Most of us are greedy to own the newest and latest and best things we can afford. But then something even better comes along and the older versions don't look so good to us anymore. However, we remember how much we paid for them and how serviceable they still are, so we're stuck. We solve the problem in various ways. Some people hoard; some people just mindlessly buy new stuff and throw out the old; some people like you might want to clear out old stuff but just can't decide what's the best thing to do, so you do nothing."

Claire opened her mouth to object, but just then both twins woke up at once, and she couldn't think of a good answer anyway. Instead, she just readied the twins for their trip home and departed with many thanks from Bethany for her help that morning.

# - 32 -
## A New Possibility

The weekend passed peacefully enough, and Claire devoted some of it to sorting out old stuff to get rid of, having been inspired by Bethany's efforts. She continued working away on this on Monday and Tuesday and decided that she'd simply store the bags of discards until one or another charitable society phoned requesting a donation and she'd then offer her discards to them. That way she wouldn't have to think about it too much. She resolved not to worry about whether or not it ended up with a grateful or needy recipient and to instead just focus on the environmental benefits of recycling.

Tuesday evening Claire made her plans and as soon as Bethany arrived on Wednesday morning, she readied herself and left the house. Twenty minutes later, she arrived at the address that she'd copied from the registration list. It was a neat little bungalow, clothed in red brick, and set well back on the lot. A winding path of paving stones artfully flanked by small bushes and patches of colorful peonies led to the welcoming red front door. A metal retracting awning adorned the front window and the whole effect was graceful and peaceful. Claire rang the doorbell, wondering what awaited her and for the first time thought that maybe she should have let Inspector McCoy know where she was going and why.

There was no answer to Claire's repeated rings at the door and her shoulders slumped in disappointment. Then she noticed the flick of curtains in the window next door and decided that it couldn't hurt to inquire there as to who lived in this charming house. That doorbell was answered readily, and a frumpy looking woman who appeared to be in her mid-sixties stared out at her.

"Ye-s?" was all she said.

"Hello. I'm looking for Mr. Fedor Kozitsky and my understanding is that he lives in that house." Claire pointed with her finger. "Have you seen him recently?"

"Why do you want him——and who are you?" the woman asked, but with more curiosity than curtness in her tone.

"Oh, I'm sorry. My name is Claire Burke and I'm a consultant working with the police on a murder investigation." Claire pulled out a card she had created to support that claim. She rarely offered these cards because it would be rather awkward if they should end up back in Inspector McCoy's hands. While it was true that he did use her as a consultant at times, he preferred to keep that relationship private, or on the "down-low" as her Aunt Gus would say.

However, by the look of this woman, Claire was fairly certain that she wouldn't fall for the kind of prevarication that had worked so well with the school receptionist, so she really had no choice.

"Oh. My name is Elsie——Elsie King. You better come in, dear. I guess you didn't know."

"Know what?" Claire asked innocently.

"Just come on in and sit down. No need to take your shoes off," she said, as Claire bent over to perform that task. The woman led her into a crowded and rather stuffy-smelling living room and pointed to a large armchair. "Just sit there, dear. It's nice and comfy. I'll get some coffee. What do you take in yours?"

From this sudden burst of effusiveness, Claire deduced that the woman was rather lonely and perhaps also a bit of a gossip. That would suit her purposes well, but Claire would have to be careful what she offered back as it might well be circulated throughout the neighbourhood.

Several minutes later, the woman returned, balancing a large tray. It held two cups, a carafe of coffee, cream and sugar and some freshly warmed and delicious smelling cinnamon rolls. "Now," she said, sitting down and pouring the coffee. "Let me tell you what I know. Fedor and his wife and daughter moved in there around twenty years ago. But a couple of years later, the wife——Sofia was her name——just disappeared. Fedor first told me that she died but I never saw any ambulance or police or anything. I had not seen her for a few days before she disappeared but then…poof!"

"Did you ever ask Fedor what really happened to her?"

"He finally admitted that she just up and left him, but he didn't want to tell his daughter that. He would rather she think that her mother had died instead of thinking that she'd abandoned her, and I could understand that. He asked me to keep it to myself so she——Marta was her name—would not find out as she grew older. But I guess it doesn't matter now since she's dead. You knew that, didn't you?" she finished, looking at Claire shrewdly.

Claire just nodded her head soberly. "What about Fedor? Is he living there now? I noticed that from the outside the house looks very well kept."

"Oh, he was a great one for fixing things. He was always working in his garden or renovating something in the house. But he lost it about three years ago. It got repossessed by the mortgage company and sold. There's a young couple living there now and they're both at work during the day and sometimes even into the evening. I don't know what they do exactly."

"Oh, I s-e-e," Claire said slowly. "Well, that complicates

things. Have you any idea where Fedor went, or if he's even still in the city?"

"Oh, I know exactly where he went."

Silence followed this remark and Claire assumed that Elsie was waiting for her to ask where. "Could you by any chance give me the address?"

"It's just a few blocks away, actually. You see…". Elsa leaned forward and lowered her voice slightly, "there's this woman about my age living in the neighbourhood who lost her husband a couple of years ago. They had a good-sized house and she didn't want to leave it, so in order to make enough money to pay for taxes and upkeep, she decided to rent out a couple of rooms."

"Oh. That was clever, I guess."

"Not in this neighbourhood," Elsie replied, an ominous tone in her voice. "People don't ever rent houses in this neighbourhood. It's just not that kind of neighbourhood."

"Well, did anyone complain?"

"Oh, I've heard people talking," Elsie replied, sniffing. "It's always a problem having itinerants around. You never know what they'll do."

"Has Fedor caused any problems?"

"Not that I know of," Elsie acknowledged grudgingly. "But he's a drinker and it got really bad after his daughter died. That's why he lost his job and his house and his new car, I've heard people say."

Claire sat back, feeling silently sorry for this poor man who'd lost first his wife and then his only child and then everything else. "I still need to talk to him," she told Elsie. "Can you please tell me exactly what his address is now?"

"It's just up the street here a couple of blocks. It's the pink, corner house just south of 51st Avenue. There's a big elm tree in front. You can't miss it."

Claire thanked her and shortly after that, she left.

# - 33 -
## A Difficult Encounter

Claire's first thought as she approached the home to which Elsie had directed her, was that it was obviously not as well cared for as Fedor's previous residence. Autumn leaves covered the grass and the front steps sagged significantly and could have used a coat of paint. She parked her car a little way down the street and thought for a minute. *Dan doesn't know what I'm doing. Nobody knows where I am. I didn't even get a chance to tell Tia, and I was afraid to share this with Al and Don in case they'd warn me off and jump in before I could interview him. It could be dangerous. Look at how that Sid Cyber situation turned out.*

Claire picked up the phone and called Inspector McCoy. She explained where she was and why she was there. Predictably, he warned her to stay out of it. He was going to check it out as soon as possible himself but he was at another crime scene right then and couldn't get away. Claire didn't answer.

Don McCoy sighed and asked, "Contact me if you need me."

"Yes."

"If there's any sign of trouble, do so."

Claire agreed, closed her cell and got out of the car. She

knocked vigorously on the door since the bell appeared to be out of order.

"Yes?" asked the tall, imperious-looking woman who opened it.

"Hello. I'm looking for Fedor Kozitsky. I understand that he's living here. Is he at home?"

The woman regarded Claire for a long moment before responding. "Yes," she finally acknowledged. "Whom shall I say is asking?"

"My name is Claire Burke and I'm a consultant for the police," Claire replied, handing over her card. "I want to speak to Mr. Kozitsky on a matter concerning his late daughter."

The woman invited Claire in without introducing herself and guided her into a small and rather dusty downstairs room that would've been called a "front parlor" in another era. It was filled with knickknacks and old-fashioned furniture and had a disused appearance. "I don't allow female visitors up to the men's rooms," she announced in a judgmental tone. Claire wondered if this was just a way to make it easier for her to listen in more easily on her boarders' juicier conversations but said nothing.

Several minutes later, the woman returned. "He's refusing to come down, but says he'll see you in his room. I guess you'll have to go up." She led the way and tapped gently at a door with the number 3 on it.

"Come in" was the slow reply, and Claire entered. It was a relatively large but very cluttered room with newspapers and dirty coffee cups and glasses covering the dresser, night table, and a small dining table. A tall, thin, and slightly stooping man with prematurely grey hair motioned her to a straight-backed chair and regarded her silently. He nodded curtly at his landlady and she scurried out, closing the door behind her.

"Mr. Kozitsky?" she inquired. He nodded and she went on. "My name is Claire Burke and I'm a police consultant looking into the murder of Stefano and Mona Amato. During the course of my investigation, your name has come to my attention. Could you please tell me what you were doing on the afternoon and evening of last June 17th?"

Fedor Kozitsky regarded her blankly but said nothing.

"Stefano apparently had a habit of wooing other men's wives, and I gather that he initially honed his skills by practicing on your daughter," Claire stated with calculated callousness.

Fedor's fists clinched, and he rose from his chair and began pacing around the room. Claire discreetly reached into her pocket and pushed a button.

Fedor reached for a Rye bottle, already two-thirds' of the way empty, and helped himself to a large drink. He took several fast swallows and turned to Claire with a snarl. "That man was a bastard. He ruined my daughter. Everything that happened to her after she got involved with him, it was all his fault. He deserved everything he got——and more."

"And Mona, his wife? Did she deserve that, too?"

"She shouldn't have interfered. She must have known what kind of a scumbag she was married to."

"And the baby?" Claire asked.

"That's what I really wanted. I wanted to take the baby. I read the birth announcement in the *Edmonton Journal,* and I knew he'd had a baby girl. He didn't deserve her. I wanted to make him know what it feels like to lose your child. But she wasn't there. That's what they both told me and after I dealt with them, I searched the house and it was true.

As he talked, Fedor was circling around the room in an increasingly agitated manner, moving various papers and books about. Watching him, Claire felt a cold chill down her back and pushed the beeper in her other pocket again. *He might not get here in time,* she thought. Then Fedor gave a sudden grunt of satisfaction. He was holding a small gun in his hands that hadn't previously been in sight.

*Just keep calm and keep talking,* Claire said to herself. Aloud, she commented, "And what would you have done with the baby?"

"I don't know. Maybe I would've just taken her home, packed my bags and driven straight south until I got to Mexico."

"What about the border? The border officials would have asked questions."

"Maybe I could've drugged her to keep her quiet and stowed her under the seat 'til I got across. Then I could've raised her myself——had a second chance at having a daughter."

"But she wasn't there that night, so you killed her parents instead," Claire summarized, hearing the faint ring of the doorbell far below.

He turned to her and raised the gun. "Tell me one more thing," she said quickly. "Why did you kill his wife? What did she ever do to you?"

"I didn't mean to, but she jumped in front of him just as I pulled the trigger."

"But why place the gun in her hands? Why make it look like she was the guilty one?"

"I would have preferred it to be him, but he fell back and twisted around onto his face when he landed. I couldn't get at his hands and I didn't want to move him."

Fedor stopped talking at that point, and Claire knew she was out of time. She started to slide out of the chair in the vain hope of scrambling for cover but just then the door burst inward, and two police officers rushed in. They yelled at Fedor to put the gun down, but he held it up to his head instead and they stopped in their tracks. A deadly silence descended on the scene and just then Inspector McCoy and Sergeant Crombie stepped through the jagged opening where the door had been.

McCoy glanced quickly at Claire to ensure she was all right and then waved the officers back. Turning to Fedor, he said, "Let's talk about this. It doesn't have to end this way. You lost a lot. I'm sure that will be considered at your trial."

"There will be no trial," Fedor replied. "I've done what I

needed to do. There's nothing left for me now." He pulled the trigger, and blood and brain matter ejected violently from his skull. Claire, at the limit of her strength, fainted.

Inspector Mc Coy turned to Sergeant McCoy. "You deal with Claire. Revive her and take her home. Get her to change and bag her clothes. Wait for me there and talk to Dan. Tell him everything. I'll join you there when I finish here. The Police Commission will have to get involved and there will be lots of paperwork. I'll order some back-up so we can guard the scene here and someone will likely go there, too, to interview you and Claire."

Turning to the two officers, he said, "You have to stay. I'm calling the Police Commission now. They'll be sending someone to take statements. Don't touch anything. We'll all just have to wait right here until we're processed."

One of the officers asked, "Aren't you going to call the coroner?"

"Of course. But he won't be able to even examine the body until designated officers arrive to witness."

Events proceeded slowly, and it was more than two hours before McCoy was able to leave the scene. An officer escorted him home first and waited for him to change so he could take McCoy's clothes. McCoy had taken a step towards Fedor before the shot and had therefore received a significant amount of brain matter on his uniform. After the officer left, he had a quick shower, still sickened and shaken himself by what had happened. Then he dressed and headed over to Claire's house. An investigating officer had already been there to get her statement and Sergeant Crombie's statement. He'd had no opportunity to change his clothes but since he'd been behind McCoy and the other officers the projectile material hadn't reached him. A woman McCoy hadn't met before was looking after the babies and Jessie and her assistant were closeted in Jessie's bedroom.

McCoy looked at Dan, who was looking grim, scared and

angry all at once. He turned to Claire and asked, "Are you okay?"

Claire nodded silently.

"You realize that because of what went down there's going to be an investigation?"

Claire nodded mutely again, and Sergeant Crombie looked worried.

"I've been asked why I involved the other officers and if I knew in advance what you were up to. I've been asked if Fedor Kozitsky would've had the opportunity to kill himself if the situation had been handled in a more orthodox manner. I've been temporarily suspended from duty and warned of the possibility of dismissal."

Claire looked miserable but continued to say nothing.

"It won't come to that, Don," Al Crombie assured him.

# - 34 -

## Proposing a New Arrangement

Several weeks had passed since the sad event, and Al Crombie and Don McCoy were enjoying a meal with Claire and Dan at their home. Dan had made his famous chili, and Claire had produced a lively Greek salad with added fresh basil leaves and arugula. She'd also baked some sour dough bread and a rhubarb coffee cake.

"It's all over," Al told them. "Don and I have been reinstated and all charges have been dismissed. The Commission has concluded that you were acting on your own, Claire, but because of your previous connection with us you called before you entered the house. They were able to get a recording of that call and it's clear from the call that Don specifically asked you not to get involved. He had reason, due to your past history, to fear that you wouldn't listen, and that's why he sent a nearby squad car, because he was unable to get away from what he was doing. Don has actually been commended for taking that step and basically saving your life. And he's also received recognition for taking up this case after it was closed because he recognized the loose threads and the need for follow through."

Claire gritted her teeth. It had happened like that because of her, not Don McCoy.

Don looked a bit sheepish and explained to Claire, "I did tell the Commission that you'd done valuable work as a consultant, getting answers for us that we couldn't have accessed otherwise. And I did tell them that I only got involved in the case because of the initial information you'd discovered on your own which convinced me that follow through was necessary. But I had to make out that Al and I were the ones doing the follow-through for the most part. I hope you understand, Claire."

Claire said nothing in reply.

She was happy to accept his credit-hogging this time because he'd put himself in a very precarious position because of her and she owed him. The four of them stopped to enjoy their meal together, then, interrupted only once by Bethany who had a question about bathing the twins. After dinner, Al cleared his throat and said, "Don and I have been talking, Claire——"

Claire and Dan were both thinking that this must be a delicate matter if Al Crombie was the spokesman. He usually took over when his superior tact was required.

"If you are to continue assisting us in our investigations from time to time——and we both hope you do because your past assistance has been invaluable——anyway, if you continue, it's going to have to be under a more formal arrangement. This may limit you in some ways, but it will also free you up in others—— greater access to resources, for example. If you need a license check, for example ,you can access it directly without going through us. And…"

Dan interrupted at this point. "I'm sorry, gentlemen, but Claire will not be engaging in any further investigations for the foreseeable future. You may ask her again, but right now she's going to focus on raising our babies for whom we waited a long time. This is not negotiable, and I will not be changing my mind. As a matter of fact, I do not even want to hear the word 'murder' in this house for a long time to come."

Claire looked at Dan and then at the two policemen and nodded her head. "Beware the anger of a patient man" was all she said.

# Recipes

### *Crustless Spinach Quiche*

Ingredients:

- 4 eggs
- 2 cups milk
- 2 cups grated cheese, preferably strong cheddar
- 1 package frozen spinach or 3 cups fresh
- 2 tablespoons flour
- ¼ teaspoon dried chili peppers (to taste)
- 1 teaspoon fresh ground nutmeg.
- ¾ teaspoon salt
- a generous sprinkling of freshly ground pepper

Method:

Preheat oven to 425 degrees Fahrenheit
Coat the inside of a large pan with oil or melted butter and place in oven to pre-heat

Place thawed and drained spinach in food processor and chop until fine. If using fresh spinach...(or...another...green: of your choice like kale or Swiss chard), wash, chop fine in processor and then microwave one to two minutes and drain any liquid. Cool before adding to other ingredients. Beat eggs until light and fluffy, add milk and stir. Beat in flour and spices vigorously to ensure they are well mixed. Stir in cheese.

Bake in oven for 15 minutes at 425 degrees. Then lower the heat to 350 degrees and bake an additional half hour. When done the quiche should be puffed, golden, firm but not dry so adjust time accordingly. Allow to rest for five minutes for further setting before cutting

Alternate Method:
Place all ingredients but cheese and spinach in blender and blend on high so flour will be well dissolved. Pour into bowl and stir in cheese and spinach. Then pour in pan and bake. For St. Patrick's Day you can blend all ingredients together. This results in a very light and very green quiche with a fine texture, perfect for Jessie, but Dan missed the chewiness of the spinach.

### *Curried Fish Soup*

In minimal oil, using a large, thick, non-stick pot, sauté 8 green cardamom pods and one tsp. dry Chana masala powder for two minutes. Then add ½ tsp. turmeric, 1 tsp. celery salt, pinch of astifida, and 1 heaping tsp. nigella seeds and sauté another minute, stirring constantly. Add 1 large chopped onion and 4 cloves garlic, finely chopped. Sauté for an additional two minutes. Stir in 2-3 tbsp. Patak's mild curry paste and 1 tsp. chopped, curried pickle. Add 2-3 cups frozen vegetables and one litre vegetable or chicken broth. Simmer for 10 minutes. Then add one pound of white fish fillets of your choice and simmer under medium low heat for a few minutes, just until fish flakes easily. Stir in 1 to 2 TB. of instant potato flakes to thicken and serve with fresh bread and a nice salad for a complete meal.

# About the Author

In her private life, Emma and her husband, Joe Pivato, have raised three children—the youngest, Alexis, having multiple challenges. Their efforts to organize the best possible life for her have provided some of the background context for this book and others in the Claire Burke series. The society that the Pivatos have formed to support Alexis in her adult years is described at **www.homewithinahome.com**.

Emma's other cozy mysteries in the Claire Burke series are entitled *Blind Sight Solution, The Crooked Knife, Roscoe's Revenge, Jessie Knows, Murder on Highway 2, Deadly Care,* and *Healthy Bodies Also Die.*

www.ingramcontent.com/pod-product-compliance
Lightning Source LLC
Chambersburg PA
CBHW070500260626
47161CB00004B/1383